Book 2 in the
*Kemmons Brothers
Baseball Series*

CHANGE
My Mind

ELLEY ARDEN

Author of *Save My Soul* and
Crashing the Congressman's Wedding

CRIMSON
ROMANCE
F+W Media, Inc.

This edition published by
Crimson Romance
an imprint of F+W Media, Inc.
10151 Carver Road, Suite 200
Blue Ash, Ohio 45242
www.crimsonromance.com

ISBN 10: 1-4405-6877-4
ISBN 13: 978-1-4405-6877-0
eISBN 10: 1-4405-6878-2
eISBN 13: 978-1-4405-6878-7

Cover art © iStockphoto.com/phototropic; 123rf

To my amazing daughter, who isn't quite old enough to read this yet, and to my sons, who protect her fiercely. The love between the three of you was the inspiration for the Parker family. Everyday I'm overcome with gratitude that you are mine.

Acknowledgments

Real life often acts as a starting point for fiction. It did for this book. While sitting in a beauty salon having my hair colored, the owner of the salon charged in with two thin, filthy dogs. The animals had been running in the street, and rather than have them hurt, she brought them in while she called their owner. As I sat there, watching this unfold, waiting for the dog's owner to arrive, a story formed in my head. What if he was famous, or at least crazy handsome and single? What if he felt gratitude enough to ask the woman out on a date? I played around with those "what ifs" for months, and eventually *Change My Mind* was born.

I wish I could thank the owner of that salon for her heroic efforts that inspired this book. Unfortunately, she passed away a couple years ago. I like to imagine her smiling down on me, happy to have been a part of something like this.

CHAPTER ONE

Nel slammed the brakes and strangled the steering wheel, fighting the urge to close her eyes, praying at least one dog cleared her Volvo's front end. Miraculously, both animals escaped disaster, dodging her car and scrambling across the empty lanes of traffic. They disappeared behind the big red sign that still made Nel's heart skip a beat more than a year after its first appearance.

Parker Properties, Inc.—as in Penelope Parker. The satisfaction of owning a real estate agency never faded.

Smoothing her right hand beneath the navy blue lapel of her wool suit coat, Nel welcomed the vibration of her heart against her hand. Of course, this bout of breathlessness was more than likely related to the kamikaze dogs…a skinny Rottweiler and a mangy golden retriever who were now eye-deep in the office's trash.

Apparently the mess-maker of the last couple weeks wasn't a raccoon.

Parking in her usual spot to the right of the front door, Nel left her briefcase and Monday's bag of bagels on the passenger seat to launch from the car with three sharp claps.

"Get outta there!" she yelled, second-guessing the brazen scare tactic when her voice hit the ice-cold air.

First the golden turned lackluster eyes on her, then the rottie. They looked sad, sick, and painfully thin. Their ribs lined the sparse fur of their bellies, and their tails hung between their legs.

"Poor babies." Nel exhaled, careful not to make any sudden movements. Hungry dogs could become mean dogs in the blink of an eye, something she should've thought about before she brought their full, agitated attention on her.

Fortunately there was no attempt to run her off, no growling or lips curling. Instead, a pitiful, phantom whine arose from one of the dogs as they both returned their noses to the garbage pile. Too bad there wasn't much edible in the black bags—a few pieces of crust from Friday's impromptu pizza lunch if they were lucky, certainly not enough to satisfy two starving dogs.

Nel turned back to the car, leaned across the front seat, and snagged the bag of bagels. Removing the carton of cream cheese, napkins, and plastic knives, she ripped a bagel in three pieces and tossed the chunks toward the animals, who jerked when the bagels thumped against the pavement.

They spied her, widening their stances, a type of standoff between foes. When Nel was sure her efforts were futile, the golden moved closer, nose to the ground, as if the bagel could be sucked through his flaring nostrils.

"Thatta girl," Nel whispered, having no idea whether or not the endearment fit. She tilted her head, looking for signs of manhood, only to roll her eyes at the awkward search.

And then the rottie moved. Five seconds later, the bagel pieces were devoured, and Nel had two new friends—friends who were desperate for more food, some water, and a good hot bath.

"What the heck is going on out here?" Rena poked her rounded face and large green eyes around the front door. "That better not be my asiago."

Nel looked at the last piece of asiago bagel in her hand and then back to Rena. "I'll buy you more."

The dogs bolted for the open door, dashing past Rena and into the office.

"Are you kidding me?" Rena yelled. "Get them out."

"They're cold." Nel picked up her pace and reached for the door, holding it open as they followed the dogs inside.

"They can't be here."

"They're strays."

The rottie tipped over a small trash can with his tail while the golden stuck her nose into an open filing cabinet.

Rena groaned. "They can't stay."

"Of course they can't stay, but I can't let them loose to get hit by a car. Come here, guys." Nel hunched over and patted palms to her knees.

To her surprise, the dogs obeyed. And as she smoothed hands over their course fur, she noticed collars and tags.

"Can you get a look at their tags?" Nel asked, holding the dogs' attention with soft, steady strokes to their bony heads.

"They're dirty, they smell; I'm sure they have fleas. I'm not touching them."

"Rena, I'm not asking you to hug them. Just bend over and peek at the tags." Some days Nel regretted hiring her best friend. The familiarity led to more than a few moments of dissonance. But hiring Rena was sort of a mercy mission. Nobody aspired to be thirty, working part-time at a pretzel stand in the mall. And Nel couldn't let Rena think that was all she was good for.

Rena rattled off a telephone number. "Remember 5293," she said, scrambling to her desk, digging through her top drawer. "Damn it! I need more pens."

"Do you eat them?" Nel teased, still rubbing the tired-looking dogs behind the ears.

"Funny. What was the number I told you to remember?"

"5293." Nel looked around the reception area. "Do we have something I can use to give them water?"

"The bucket the cleaners use for mopping," Rena said, holding the desk phone to her ear.

"I'm not going to let them drink out of something with chemical residue."

"They were eating out of the garbage. I hardly think it matters."

It mattered. They didn't deserve to be subjected to more harm. By the looks of them, they'd been through so much already. Nel stared into their sad eyes and smiled while she made a mental tour of the office, settling on a plastic bowl full of blank nametags in the supply closet.

"No answer, and the mailbox is full. Now what?" Rena perched on the edge of her desk.

"Get me the plastic bowl from the supply closet filled with water, and then we'll think of something."

Nel hated to call the shelter…actually, she refused. There were plenty of rescues around town who would ensure the dogs were rehabbed and given good homes. Before she reached out to one of them, she would do whatever she could to find the animals' owner.

The rottie slumped to the hardwood floor, leaving Nel petting the golden. With a tiny movement, Nel moved her hand lower on the golden's neck, combing her nails through the fur, inching closer to the buckle. If she could just get a good look at the tags …

"Where do you want it?" Rena walked toward them with the bowl.

"Right here." Nel gestured to the floor at her feet and stepped back while unlatching the collar in one fluid movement. She glanced at the tags in her hand. "The golden's name is Blackjack." The telephone number Rena called was etched below the name. Beneath that tag nestled a county-issued tag. "I wonder if they can trace the dogs by this number."

It was worth a phone call.

While the dogs drank, Nel made the call, and sure enough, the ID number on Blackjack's tag led to the address used to license the dog—an address that wasn't far away. Nel glanced at the dogs, resting on the drenched floor, noses centimeters from the water bowl, and satisfaction squared her shoulders. She was going to get these boys home, and home was…she Googled the address, nearly dropping the phone when she looked at the satellite map.

"Oh. My. God." She pointed to her cell phone screen. "Rena, these dogs belong at Castle Chaos."

Castle Chaos was the single greatest piece of residential architecture in the South Hills. The kind of property that could put a small, struggling real estate agency on the radar of every other agency in Pittsburgh.

"I suppose that's fitting," Rena sneered. "Decrepit animals belong in a decrepit house."

Nel waved off the cynicism. "That house is worth millions."

"To a vampire in Transylvania."

"I love that house."

"You also love slasher movies. Your taste is questionable."

Nel stuck out her tongue rather than defend her cinematic choices once again. "I'm going to drive the dogs over there."

"In your car?"

"No, in yours." She cast Rena a sarcastic grin and clapped to get the dogs' attention.

Everything happened for a reason. These dogs, coming from that house, now being in her office, had *business opportunity* written all over it. Maybe the old, rich guy who owned the place would be so thankful to see his dogs returned safely, he'd admit he couldn't keep up with the house anymore, and he'd agree to let Nel be the listing agent. She smiled as she slid behind the wheel of her car with the dogs safely in the backseat.

One of these days, Nel Parker was going to look back on this moment and remember it as the moment when everything changed.

• • •

Elevator music on the other end of the cell phone threatened to drive Grey insane. If his teeth weren't being ground to bits out of frustration, they'd be chattering, shaking along with the rest of his chilled body. *How hard was it to get a boiler fixed in the dead of winter?*

"We can have the technician there tomorrow morning, tomorrow afternoon at the latest."

Apparently pretty damn hard.

"That's the best you can do?" Grey growled.

"I'm afraid so, sir. Looking at past maintenance records I can tell you…that particular boiler is a special case."

Of course it was, because Grey's father never did anything reasonable.

With a grunt of concession he ended the call, sliding the cell phone across the marble counter, careful not to touch the ice-cold stone and add to his misery. He knew returning this house to some semblance of glory was going to be backbreaking work, but he never expected to freeze to death before he drove a single nail.

Scrubbing his palms together, Grey tried to generate some heat; thankful for the beard he left growing long after the Argonauts were eliminated from the postseason. Anonymity was the initial reason for the thick black facial hair, but now there was a practical purpose for not packing a razor or shaving cream. He needed warmth, but he needed more than the beard and the six-burner gas stove were supplying.

A limestone fireplace loomed over the great room, offering an easy solution now that the boiler wasn't going to be fixed until tomorrow. Grey didn't like the idea of using a fireplace that hadn't been serviced in God-only-knew how long, but he'd have to take his chances.

First things first. He grabbed a yellowed, brittle newspaper off the pile he had collected from the front stoop. With a twist, the paper turned into a makeshift torch, and he lit it with the blue gas flame. After turning off the stove, he carried the burning paper into the great room, where he ducked his head beneath the massive limestone blocks and reached an arm into the flue. He hoped the draft would carry the smoke from the paper up the chimney, and out of the house. *That* was the sign he was waiting for as he hunched over, holding his breath.

For once, since he arrived at this empty, sorry house, something miraculously went his way. The smoke curled in ribbons up the chimney and Grey dropped the newspaper to the firebox floor. Now, all he needed was some wood; and from the looks of the overgrown grounds surrounding the house, he wouldn't have a problem finding it.

Making his way through the cavernous, sparsely decorated icebox, he made another trip to the basement; this time ignoring the mammoth boiler and heading for the dingy workroom, where he noticed an axe propped against the cement block wall. Trudging back up the stairs and through the house with axe in tow, his anger grew until the combination of movement and emotion had him breaking into a sweat. *Fuck you, Dad*, he thought for about the millionth time since the bastard ran off to Bermuda—taking Grey's longtime girlfriend along for the ride.

He gripped the axe so hard his knuckles screamed with pain, and for a moment he thought about taking a swing at the ornate trim lining the backdoor. Fortunately for his already-lengthy to-do list, the axe stayed at his side, and his anger peaked. It didn't pass so much as it returned to whatever dark hole Grey stashed it in; leaving him with labored breath and a clenched jaw.

At least he wasn't cold anymore.

Outside in the wind, he made his way through a crunching layer of frozen grass and leaves, to the back of the property where an empty dog run formed a visible boundary between this property and the sloping hillside beyond. He didn't know what happened to the dogs. The lawyer for the estate made no mention of them, so Grey figured his dad had given them away. Then again, maybe he took them to Bermuda. Maybe they were on the plane when it went down—just like Dad and Lindsay.

Grey flinched. He cared more about losing those dogs than he did about losing his father and the woman he had expected to someday marry. With both hands wrapped around the grip of the axe, Grey swung hard at one of the brittle tree trunks littering the frozen ground, feeling the burn in his shoulder and the vibration clear up to his elbows. He stood there, axe lodged in wood, wondering how he got from centerfield in Nashville's brand-new ballpark, to the backyard of a house he didn't want to own. And once again, he was reminded of how his father fucked up everyone's lives.

Yeah? Well, this was where the chain stopped.

Swinging the axe again, noticing less of a protest from his body, Grey reminded himself the house was key to repairing some of the damage his father had caused. All he had to do was fix it up and sell it off, for as close to a million dollars as possible. He swung the axe again, praying to God he could manage the miracle before he needed to report for spring training in a little more than two months. *Two months.* He squeezed his eyes shut as he swung the axe again.

He was crazy. Anyone who discovered what he was doing would agree. This wasn't a job for one man, and yet Grey couldn't figure out how to let anyone else in; how to trust them enough to relinquish the tiniest bit of control. There was too much at stake. He needed to limit the amount of money spent on the renovations, maximize the return on his investment, and sweat out the anger he felt toward his father—and the guilt he felt for not being man enough to stand up to him.

Maybe the daunting task was some sort of self-imposed punishment. After what Grey had done, turning his back on his brother's professional advice and personal support in order to maintain a half-assed relationship with the world's worst dad? This wasn't nearly as harsh of a punishment as he deserved.

Two shrill barks ripped through the frosty silence, and before Grey could turn around he was hit from behind.

"Holy shit." He dropped the axe to rough the dogs behind the ears. "Where'd you come from?"

"They were in my garbage."

She couldn't have been more than five feet tall, standing at the top of the cement walk that led from the front of the house to the back patio. She was dwarfed by the iron gazebo trellises to her left, but there was something formidable about her. Maybe it was the fact that she stood strong despite being sorely underdressed for the current weather conditions. Dressed in nothing but a navy blue pantsuit with her blonde curls whipping around her wind-reddened, heart-shaped face, she was the last sort of thing he expected to see in his father's backyard.

Grey opened his mouth to speak or breathe, but the cold air tightened his throat and chest.

The dogs ran back to her.

"I'm sorry. They belong here, don't they? The county gave me the address based on their license numbers." She bent forward, wrapping each hand around a dog's neck. She looked even smaller in their presence.

Grey blinked, swallowed, and nodded his head; hoping to generate some meaningful thoughts and words to counteract the surprise of seeing the dogs and her...whoever she was. "They belong here."

"Good." She smiled. "I'm sure they're happy to be home. It looks like they've been lost for a while." She patted their thin sides, and anger pinched in his chest. Once again his father's propensity for living a disposable life had hurt more than him.

"Yeah, I..." Grey walked toward her, not knowing what to say exactly, but not wanting to seem rude after she brought the dogs home. He stopped, wondering how close was too close; close enough to be recognized. "I don't know how long they've been gone. I just got here myself."

"Oh." She looked disappointed. Her forehead crinkled and her eyebrows bunched. But when she wound her arms around her body, he figured the cold had finally caught up with her. "You don't live here?"

"No." He was uncomfortable with questions, so he clapped his hands and gestured for the dogs, hoping without them, she'd feel inclined to leave.

"I'm sorry to bother you. Is the homeowner inside? I can knock and let him know I've returned the dogs."

"I'll take it from here." Maybe she was sincere, but it felt like she was digging. Then again, Grey suspected everyone of having an ulterior motive. He'd never been proven wrong. Dressed in a suit like that, she was either an overly nosey neighbor on her lunch break or someone with a business interest in the estate.

Grey didn't want to deal with either.

She hesitated, tightening her arms around her chest, looking over her shoulder at the house, and then back at him. "Are they renovating?"

Clear blue eyes widened and the corner of her lips hitched, like his answer was something she highly anticipated. If he weren't such a miserable bastard, he would've smiled at her enthusiasm—if only because she was so damn pretty.

"I parked behind the dumpster," she continued. "Dumpsters usually signify a reno." She pushed a clump of golden curls off her face and treated him to a blinding smile. "My name's Nel Parker. You may have heard of me or my agency, Parker Properties. I'm a real estate agent, and houses are my passion. I'd love to see what's going on inside…I've admired this property for years."

Yeah, she was pretty, but she was pushy, too.

Grey watched the dogs tear up the hill to the dog run. "Maybe another time. I need to get them taken care of."

"Oh. Of course, I'll just leave you with my card, and you can have the owner get in touch with me at his convenience."

Don't hold your breath, Grey thought as he extended an arm and accepted her card in his hand. Her fingernails brushed the skin he could've sworn was frozen and beyond capable of feeling anything but the pain of frostbite. Instead, the light touch thawed him, and he wrapped warm fingers around the card, squeezing until the card creased; feeling unnerved by his reaction to a perfect stranger.

"Have a good day." She looked around him up the hill to the romping dogs. "Be good boys; stay put." She laughed at herself, and a gust of icy wind lifted her hair, tossing it forward, framing her face like a golden headdress.

Damn. Grey watched her turn and walk away. With her shoulders back, hips swinging and hair whipping out of control, she was like nothing he'd ever seen. Too pretty and too tiny to be taken seriously, and yet he had the feeling she wasn't someone to mess with.

So why was the idea of messing with her so appealing?

CHAPTER TWO

That was a bust.

Nel knew better than to leave a potential listing without a firm commitment for a follow-up appointment or telephone call. Passing her business card off to God-only-knows-who and expecting a call from the homeowner was likely to be as successful as cold calling. She hated cold calling. The thought alone prompted a shudder as she wound her arms tighter around her waist and hurried to the car, still idling in the mansion's driveway. But what else could she have done? She wasn't about to throw herself at the mercy of Grizzly Adams just to gain entrance to the house. Even if it was a glorious house—the most glorious house she'd ever seen. And now that she'd seen it up close, she was downright salivating.

She needed to know more about the renovations. Was the house destined for sale? Had it bypassed the market and changed hands without her knowing? What if the current owner intended to stay? So many questions. Fortunately she didn't have to throw herself at anyone's mercy to get the answer to one of those questions.

Back at the office, Nel flipped open her laptop and powered up the machine while she sipped piping-hot green tea, trying to chase away the lingering chill. Rena was on the phone. By her snippy tone, Nel could tell the caller was someone barely tolerable. When it came to Rena, that list was long.

"I'll relay the message. Thank you for calling." She hung up the phone, yanked her hair at the roots and screamed.

Only one man could prompt such a reaction. "What did *he* want?"

"To invite you to a home-buying seminar he's conducting at the Westin next week. He thought you could use the exposure." Rena made a gagging sound around the last word. "Will Fortune is a hemorrhoid-riddled asshole."

Nel couldn't have said it better herself, and the juvenile slight made her giggle…until she remembered the asshole was also the owner of the top-producing agency in town.

And she helped him get there.

"Say it," Rena demanded, spinning around in her desk chair, slapping her hands to her corduroy-covered knees.

"Say what?"

"Your face is bunched like a prune. You're holding back some serious emotion; so say it. Get it out."

Nel opened her mouth, sucked a mouthful of air, and let loose with a barrage of insults that started with 'mother' and ended with her shouting, "I hate Will Fortune!"

Her pulse had quickened, her throat was sore, and beads of sweat trickled down her back. The man made her blood boil.

Rena wrapped an arm around Nel's shoulder. "Good girl. Feels better, doesn't it?" And when she laughed, Nel had to admit releasing her anger felt pretty damn good.

She shook her head and leaned against Rena's arm. "I wish he'd stop calling. He's only rubbing it in."

"Because you humiliated him in front of his office staff. He's got to re-inflate his balls somehow."

Nel swatted at her, laughing. "You're bad."

"I'm also right, aren't I?"

"Yeah, you're right." Nel knew the phone calls wouldn't stop until she proved to Will that leaving The Fortune Agency to start her own company wasn't the act of a disgruntled girlfriend, but the act of a talented businesswoman kept from reaching her full potential by the thumb of a sexist pig. "I'm not going to pout. We have work to do."

Thirty minutes later, with the help of the tax assessment website, Nel had a last name to go along with the house: Kemmons.

"So let me get this straight. Ten years ago, somebody paid nine hundred thousand dollars for that house, and last month somebody got it for free? That should tell you it's a hellhole."

Nel stared at the transaction amounts and dates on the screen. "That only tells me somebody didn't want the house anymore, so they gave it away…or they died."

She opened another browser screen and Googled the first owner on the list, Francis Kemmons. Her eyes settled on the most popular search result: *Bermuda Plane Crash Claims Notorious Baseball Business Man's Life*. "Bingo." She clicked.

"So he died," Rena said over Nel's shoulder. "And the other Kemmons inherited the place."

"Looks that way." Her pulse quickened. If she were a betting woman, she'd put everything she had on the house getting ready for sale.

She scanned the article, catching sentences here and there about a self-made man who acted as agent to his sons' baseball careers. She wasn't interested. She didn't care how he got his money. She only cared that he made enough to buy a keystone property that was now on her radar to sell.

"I bet one of these sons owns it now." She toggled back to the tax assessment page. "Greyson."

"Weird name."

"I don't care what his name is, I just want to know if he's selling." Nel typed the name into the search box and waited for the page to load. "The lumberjack I talked to today wasn't much help in the way of information, and I totally…"

Six thumbnail images topped the search results page. In all but one shot, dark, familiar eyes stared back at her.

"You totally what?" Rena nudged her. "You wanna get with that?" She whistled. "Because I do. I would strip…"

"Rena," Nel interrupted, raising a hand over her shoulder for emphasis. "That's him."

"Who?"

"The lumberjack. I mean, he has a thick, nasty beard now, and he was wearing a stocking cap instead of a ball cap; but those eyes…" Her gaze settled on the pale curves of his lips. "And that mouth…" she swallowed something uncomfortable. "It's definitely him."

"Lucky dog," Rena whistled. "And I'm talking about you, not the actual dogs curled up with him right now."

Nel had to disagree. There wasn't anything lucky about it. The guy was hardly pliable. He certainly didn't seem interested in anything she had to say that morning. He looked at her more like a curious annoyance than a legitimate business prospect— something she was painfully used to—and halfway through their so-called conversation, she was just thankful he hadn't thrown her off the property.

"I thought he was part of the work crew," Nel mused. "He wore flannel; he had an axe."

"Wait…" Rena gripped Nel's shoulders "…he's a rich, hot, professional athlete with manual labor skills? Excuse me while I change my underwear."

Nel winced. "He's grumpy."

"His father died." Rena squealed. "Maybe he needs to be consoled."

Nel doubted that very much. There'd been a steeliness in his black eyes that told her he wasn't open for small talk, let alone consoling. "He's not my type." Which was an incredible understatement. Nel didn't do powerful, successful men…at least not anymore. All they ever did was take what she could give and steamroll what she wanted.

And she wanted to list that house.

The question was, was she willing to do what it would take to get it?

•••

Closing her trunk on a fifteen-pound bag of dog food, Nel was convinced she'd gone overboard. They weren't her dogs. She didn't even know what kind of food they ate…a box of treats would've been enough. As it was, she looked like Santa Paws with a trunkful of dog supplies, all in the hopes of gaining entry to Castle Chaos. Certainly he had too much on his mind, what with losing his father and renovating the house, to take care of the dogs properly. She was doing him a favor. Sure, she was doing herself a big one, too, but what was the harm if everyone won? *None*, she thought with a nod, and it was the boost she needed to get herself to his driveway.

Getting out of the car was another story.

As the only girl in a family of four sons, she knew a thing or two about being ballsy, and normally she didn't think twice about whatever gutsy action was needed to get what she wanted. So why was she hesitating now? Maybe she was afraid of him. She stared up at the gargantuan stone house and thought about the man inside; large, dark, and distant. If he told her to get out, she'd go without hesitation. After all, what were the chances a man like that was going to listen to anything she had to say?

Oh, God. Nel caught movement out of the corner of her eye, and sure enough the object of her mental meanderings appeared from the far side of the dumpster, stocking cap in place, flannel shirt blowing in the winter wind. Underneath, a white T-shirt clung to his flat abs, and Nel's stomach tumbled. Their eyes met, prompting a wave of panic which Nel swallowed down with a whimper. She could do this. She'd dealt with impossible people before. She had something he needed—whether he realized it or not. Her job wasn't to do anything more than convince him to sell this house and list with her. Easy.

He rounded the front of her car, her heartbeat echoing louder with each step he took. When he came to a stop at the driver's side door, he shrugged, like he was trying to figure out what the hell she was doing.

Funny, she was trying to figure out the same thing.

He tapped on the window, motioning for her to roll down the glass, and she clenched her teeth; holding back a groan as she eliminated the barrier between them.

"Hi," she managed, despite the clog of conflicting emotion in her throat.

He didn't soothe her with a greeting of his own. He simply stood there; large and quiet.

Nel looked beyond him to the house. "I was worried about the dogs and wanted to do something to help…I brought food."

He nodded. "I appreciate that."

Praise be to God, he sounded sincere. Nel's exhale was a little too vigorous, and she glanced at him for any sign he caught on to her nervousness and subsequent relief.

When he grinned, her nerves returned.

"I bet you'd like payback for your generosity." One black brow lifted until it brushed the edge of his stocking cap. "Something like a tour of the house, right?" He nodded, so damn sure he had her pegged.

Arrogance in a man usually rubbed her the wrong way, but this time it didn't. How could it when the swagger of a professional athlete was masked with a beard, cloaked in flannel, and topped with a knit cap? Like this, it was easy to forget he was somebody much of the world would coddle to, admire, and envy.

She'd do none of the above—except take him up on the house tour.

Nel squared her shoulders and chin. "If you're offering to give me a tour of the house, I accept. That way I can also help you carry in the food."

He sniffed, puffed out his chest a bit, and hitched his thumbs in his jean pockets. "Do I look like I need help carrying a bag of dog food?"

Typical male. Quick to defend his manhood when in question. She wrinkled her nose, clearly not impressed. "I brought more than food. So unless you want to make multiple trips, you should deign to let me help."

He blinked a few times, and she wondered if he was trying to figure out what "deigned" meant—a thought that prompted a little chuckle she kept hidden with a bite to her cheek. He glanced into her backseat.

"It's all in the trunk," she said, rolling up the window and pushing out of the car, feeling very pleased with the direction things were going. It was time to up her game. "I didn't know exactly what to get, so I got a little of everything." She opened the trunk and waved a hand over the contents. "If there's anything you don't want, I can take it back or donate it to a rescue."

"You're a dog lover?"

"And a shrewd business woman." She sucked a mouthful of air as fortification. "Mr. Kemmons, I want to list your house."

• • •

Grey dragged his gaze from the pet-shop-in-a-trunk to level narrow eyes on the blonde spitfire beside him. "How do you know my name and that this is my house?"

"Allegheny County tax assessments."

He grunted, a feeling of unease hardening his muscles. "What else do you know about me?"

"That once this baseball season starts, you'll be too busy to be tied to a home like this."

Great. He roughed a palm over his face until his fingers tucked beneath his stocking cap, and he pushed the hat back on his head to release some steam.

It was always the same. People knowing every little detail about him before he knew anything significant about them. Yeah, yeah, he'd heard it all, how it was a fair trade for the money he made and the envious game he played, but as the years went by, he wasn't so sure.

"Listen, I don't want anyone to know I'm here or what I'm doing," he warned. "It's nobody's business but mine."

"And your realtor's." She grinned. "I'll be completely discreet. Nobody will know this house is getting ready for listing until the sign post is driven into the front yard."

He tugged his cap back in place, wishing he could pull it over his eyes and make her go away. But by the gleam in her eyes and the set of her jaw, he could tell she wasn't going anywhere. She was a realtor; sniffing around his property. And here he thought she was a baseball groupie, sniffing around him.

Huh. He'd been bamboozled by a pixie in a wool suit with a trunkful of marrow bones.

"You need me, Mr. Kemmons." She pressed her pouty lips together and nodded, making her sunny curls dance.

A spark ignited his belly, and he fidgeted against the burning, shifting his weight from one foot to the other.

"I know houses, and I know this market," she continued. "If it's a quick sale you want, I'll make it happen. If it's top-dollar you need, I'll make that happen, too."

What if he wanted to find her naked in his bed? Could she arrange that, too?

He slammed shut his eyes and pinched the bridge of his nose out of pure disgust. This wasn't the time or place to be making decisions with his dick, but he was overworked and under the gun, and she was apparently an easy distraction.

This whole thing had trouble written all over it.

Still, if she could deliver on promises to sell quick and high, couldn't he manage a little more trouble? Partnering with her would save him the hassle of finding someone else. If a wayward attraction was his biggest concern, he could control his urges for two months. Hell, with as much physical labor as he had facing him, there wouldn't be energy to spare. Besides, after witnessing her assertiveness firsthand, he had a feeling she'd rather bust his balls than stroke him kindly.

Frustration rumbled in his throat as he shook his head free of the ridiculousness. "Let me show you the house before you commit to something you'll regret." Grey leaned over the trunk, scooped up the bag of food and headed toward the house, half hoping she didn't follow.

When he turned around at the door, she was hot on his heels.

CHAPTER THREE

It was the most God-awful thing she'd ever seen.

Nel maneuvered around Grey's massive frame, made wider by the bag of dog food hoisted over his shoulder, to get a closer look at the inside of the house. She closed her eyes, opened them again, and squeezed the pet supplies she was carrying tighter to her chest.

Rena was right, and Nel was never going to live it down.

A crimson and evergreen floral pattern papered the great room, making Nel want to shield her eyes. She looked away from the busy walls, hoping to find relief in weathered, hardwood floors beneath her feet. Instead, she stood on a patch of gaudy jade marble, which separated the foyer from the rest of the room. If the hideous decorating ended there, they'd be in decent shape. But no such luck. Nel swallowed a groan. The marble gave way to black and white, twelve-by-twelve ceramic tiles, the pattern blurring her vision as it went on and on into the deeper recesses of the home; like a mind-boggling, three-dimensional mosaic picture meant to leave viewers scratching their heads. If Nel's hands were free, she'd definitely be scratching.

What the hell were they thinking?

Nothing matched. The horrid green marble continued to the hearth of the giant limestone fireplace, which was flanked by humongous, gauche gold sconces and topped with an entirely too-high black lacquered mantle. There was nothing classic or elegant about the room, unless one counted the ornate wainscoting painted mustard yellow.

Nel wasn't one of those people.

She gnawed her bottom lip in an attempt to keep quiet, until the shock had passed and she could temper her words.

"I know it needs some work," Grey said.

That was an understatement. She watched him lumber into the great room toward the fireplace, where he leaned the bag of dog food against the heinously wallpapered accent wall, and lifted a poker from a collection of iron tools. He stabbed the glowing wood, releasing orange sparks and smoke. She was just about to say something—anything—to interject some hope back into her mood, when barking echoed through the house.

Nel turned in time to see the dogs careening around a far corner, slipping on the tile, heading straight for Grey…then they caught sight of her. She had only a second to brace against the front door before four paws pressed into her belly and two long noses poked into her armful of goodies.

"Down," Grey bellowed.

The dogs jumped; Nel jumped, too. She'd been so preoccupied with the house, she'd forgotten how on edge Grey made her feel. His rough tone of voice and the goose pimples on her skin were a vivid reminder.

"Blackjack, Joker, come."

And they did.

She was happy to see Grey sink to his knees and praise them for listening with vigorous rubs behind the ears; but his booming voice still rang in her ears, and the goose pimples lingered.

He wasn't going to be easy to work with, was he? Another man who'd steamroll her ideas and think his way was best. She'd end up covertly manipulating the situation so that what really was best got done, but in the end, he'd get all the credit. Just like Will Fortune. Her shoulders sagged.

"Why don't we put that stuff in the kitchen? They might try to snatch it off the counter, but they haven't figured out how to open cupboards yet." His lips lifted until the corners disappeared beneath the edges of his beard.

And just like that, she thought maybe she was wrong. Maybe he wasn't anything like Will. Maybe he'd listen and give her the reins. She was the professional, after all.

Following him through the great room, Nel counted checkered tiles. "It's pretty ghastly, you know?"

He grunted a laugh. "Yeah, well, you should've seen it with furniture. Empty, it's tolerable. I figure I can paint the shit-yellow walls and be in good shape; concentrate on this."

They turned a corner and Nel stepped into the ugliest kitchen she'd ever seen. The green marble from the foyer repeated on the countertops. The cupboards gleamed glossy black. Gold hardware, faucets, and fixtures completed the garish design.

"It's a gut," she whispered, eyes wide.

"Well, I don't know about a gut. I'm going to update the appliances and change out the marble at least."

At least. She blinked and looked away from the kitchen horror to the flannel-clad man, leaning against an enormous butcher block island in the center of the room. He was in complete denial.

She stepped forward to the opposite side of the island, where she emptied her arms of the pet supplies. "Did you have a list price in mind?" Maybe he wasn't renovating so much as hoping to clean it up and dump it off.

"I own it free and clear. I don't care what it's listed at. As long as I walk away with a million, I'll be happy."

She gagged on disbelief. In its current state, she'd be lucky to list it at eight-hundred-thousand and get seven.

"What?" He straightened, narrowing his eyes. "You think that's too much?"

"I think it's overly ambitious unless you plan to take down the wallpaper, rip out the flooring, and rebuild this kitchen from scratch."

He yanked the hat from his head, freeing a mess of black curls. "I don't have time for that. I need this place ready to list in two months."

"That's plenty of time with the right crew. I know…"

"No crew. Whatever work needs to be done, I'll do it." He tossed the stocking cap on top of the bag of dog food as if he were throwing down a gauntlet. His darkened eyes never left her face.

It figured, didn't it? Nel found a way to prove her capabilities, and she had to wrestle a stubborn man to succeed. *Mental wrestling*, she corrected, dropping her gaze from the shadows of his face to the girth of his body and his wide-set hands. Definitely not physical wrestling. He was twice her size. Everywhere. And he was no doubt strong in a baseball bat, axe-wielding sort of way. Heat washed over her face, and she forced herself to look him in the eyes, to take back some control.

"If…" she paused for dramatic effect, stressing the 'if' "…you listen to me, you'll make your million dollars."

"Is that so?" He splayed his palms against the countertop and leaned in, closer and closer until she could smell the clash of winter wind and charred wood on his flannel shirt. There was something wild and dirty about the scent; something that made her pulse quicken. "Can you guarantee me that?"

She shouldn't. There were no guarantees in real estate, but as usual, she hated the idea of backing down more than she hated the idea of breaking her back to make the impossible happen.

Pressing her belly into the cold countertop, Nel lifted her chin and closed the already narrowed gap between their faces. "I guarantee it," she said, despite the twinge of doubt burrowing behind her eyes.

Grey pushed away, walking a circle in the empty area Nel would call a spacious eat-in kitchen when she wrote up promotional material. "You need to see the rest of the house," he said, scratching at his beard.

"Okay."

"Six bathrooms." He threaded his fingers through the jet-black hair on his head and lifted his face to the beamed ceiling. "You're going to tell me those all have to be gutted, too, aren't you?"

She bit her bottom lip at his despair. God, he was cute when he was flustered. "Probably."

And then he growled. Growling wasn't cute. It was either sexy in a predatory way, or it was scary in a domineering way. She didn't want to think of him being either.

"Follow me."

Despite her reservations, she did, but not before she patted a hand to her hip and summoned the dogs who'd been dozing by the fire. She might be easily led astray by her own ambition, but she was no dummy. If she was going to do battle with this stranger, she was going to have a couple friends by her side.

• • •

Grey had been so damn tired and slept so deeply, that he almost forgot the nightmare facing him when he woke. Staring at Nel's loopy letters strung together on a paper towel, he was reminded; no amount of black coffee was going to help him face her list.

Swallowing a scalding mouthful anyway, he acclimated himself to the list he was too angry to read more than once last night. After Nel's reaction to the house tour, he should've expected most of the items she listed; things like removing the wallpaper, installing hardwoods, and pretty much gutting the kitchen and baths. But some things surprised him, like replacing the banister and painting the garage floor. And some things were downright picky, like changing the outlet covers and getting rid of all ceiling fans.

Shit. By his estimation it would take one hundred grand and six months to cross everything off the list.

He read over the list again and came to the conclusion that Nel was a slave driver. And while his fingers slid inward, crumpling the towel beneath his hand, readying to defer from her plan of attack, his brain reminded him she had guaranteed one million dollars if he followed her lead.

Did he have a choice here? Apparently not, if he wanted to make a million dollars, and not after seeing proof of what she was saying. When she whipped out her smartphone to show him million-dollar home after million-dollar home, none of them anywhere near the shape of this, he knew he was already beaten.

Flattening his palm over the list, he decided to stop wasting time second-guessing her. He didn't have time to complain. He also didn't have time for a ringing cell phone, but he slid the black rectangle closer so he could see who was calling.

Jordon. Maybe the baby was born. It wasn't every day a man became an uncle, so despite being annoyed by both Nel's list and the distraction, Grey answered.

"Did she pop?" he asked, getting right to the point, hoping to keep the call short and sweet.

"You're an uncle, man. Braydon James was born at five this morning. He's a complete beast—a tank. Ten pounds of strapping baby boy, and, man, the set of lungs on this kid." Jordon laughed.

Grey smiled. It was nice to hear his brother happy. "Congratulations." And he meant it so much it hurt, pinching in his chest. "How's Maggie?"

"Perfect. She never broke a sweat. Stronger than I'd ever be. She's sleeping now, but I'll tell her you asked about her. She'll appreciate it." A tiny squeal punctuated Jordon's sentence, and kissing sounds followed.

For some reason, the mental image that went along with the sounds made Grey wince. It wasn't that he was a killjoy. After everything, Jordon deserved things to go his way. Wasn't that why Grey was breaking his back here in Pittsburgh? But Grey did better with other people's happiness when it wasn't so in his face.

The baby squealed again.

"Sounds like you're being paged," Grey said. "I don't want to keep you, man."

"Hold on a minute. You're not getting off this phone until you promise me you'll come to North Carolina. How about next week?"

The fact that Grey's face hadn't relaxed since his last wince saved him the energy of wincing again. He glanced around the great room and then at Nel's list. "I'm kind of busy."

"It's the off-season. What could you possibly be doing that's more important than meeting your nephew?"

Righting an age-old wrong. Getting back the money Dad stole from you. Showing you how damn sorry I am for choosing him instead of you. Yep, that about summed it up, but Grey couldn't admit those things to Jordon. Jordon would balk and say it was best to let sleeping dogs lie. He'd never take a dime of retribution from Grey—especially not outright. After all, it wasn't Grey who stole the money in the first place, so cutting Jordon a personal check for a million dollars wasn't going to fly.

But it was Grey who inherited what was left of the dirty money, which was all tied up in this house. Blood money…money Grey lived on when he was under his father's charismatic spell…money that served no other purpose than to feed a man's ego while he tore his three sons apart. Grey had no idea how to mend the rift with Tag, but he'd do whatever it took to get this money back in Jordon's hands, even if that meant being sneaky. There was no way he'd let this sleeping dog lie.

Speaking of dogs …

Grey hadn't considered them when he answered the call, but now that he did, he worried they'd bark and cause Jordon to ask more questions.

"I hate to cut you short, bro, but I gotta go." He took a deep breath and exhaled, knowing that excuse alone wouldn't be enough to appease Jordon, so he added, "I kind of got myself into something I don't want to talk about now, but I'll give you details later."

Jordon took a turn exhaling. "As your agent, that scares the hell out of me. As your brother, I'm going to trust you know what you're doing."

Looking at Nel's asinine list, Grey wasn't so sure.

Four hours later with blisters burning his palms and only half of the ceramic tile in the great room demoed, he was sure this was the worst idea he'd ever had, and listening to the Fairy Princess of Doom was the second worst. If things kept going like this, he wouldn't be able to hold a bat in two months, let alone make a million dollars on this house.

Flipping the handle of the sledgehammer, sending the tool smashing to the ground, Grey gave up and went to check on the dogs, who were shut in the den to keep them out from under foot. After he filled their water bowls and played fetch until they were good and worn out, he dragged his sore, tired body back down to the great room.

He prepared himself to see the mess he'd left, but he wasn't prepared to see Nel. She was pushing a broom over the shattered tiles, gathering the chaos into one corner of the room. Her blonde curls looped through the back of a baseball hat, and a gray sweatshirt hung low on her blue jean-covered legs. He couldn't help but smile when he noticed the work boots. She was something else. He couldn't exactly define what that something else was, so he didn't try. He stepped forward, hitting a creaking floorboard, and she looked up with a startled smile.

"Progress," she said, a sparkle in her eyes. "It's exciting."

He could've argued with her assessment. The mess didn't look like progress to him. It looked worse than when he started, like with every hit of the hammer he lost himself another grand. But she was standing there, leaning on the broom, looking around the room with the biggest smile on her face, and he didn't feel like trouncing her delusions. He told himself it was about the money. If he kept Nel happy, she'd make good on her guarantee.

Spreading his fingers, stretching his sore hands, Grey walked toward her. "I still have a long way to go."

"I know. That's why I'm here. I would've been here earlier, but I had an open house, and then I had to run home to change."

"You don't have to be here."

"Yes, I do. You're too stubborn to hire a crew, and you're crazy if you think you can finish the list by yourself in two months. If things get bad, my friend Rena can help, too. She's also my office manager, so she'll stay quiet about who you are and what you're doing."

Nel pushed the broom again, creating a cloud of dust that sort of consumed her. She wrinkled her nose and sneezed a few times, and he found himself smiling again. Maybe that was why he didn't fight her being here, and he didn't fight the idea of her friend helping out, too. As long as they worked and worked hard—and kept their mouths quiet about the project—he could use the help.

Picking up the sledgehammer, Grey moved away from her so ceramic shrapnel wouldn't do her damage, but instead of swinging the hammer, he watched her bend over and tip a box on its side to collect debris. He tried to make out the curves of her ass through the baggy sweatshirt, knowing it was a dangerous game. He had too much work to do to indulge in distraction.

"Do you have gloves? Gloves would make this easier." She tossed him a look over her shoulder and then straightened, brushing the dust from her palms with a few swipes.

"On the mantel." It was too high for her to reach, but he doubted she'd ask for help. He should offer, but that would involve him moving closer. Grey liked to keep his distance.

He swung the hammer then, hard and loud, letting the vibration shake his head from his ass. He swung again, but couldn't stop himself from glancing in her direction, catching her on tiptoes, reaching for the gloves.

It struck him then, how different she was from Lindsay. That had to be why he found her so fascinating. Tying himself down to his high school sweetheart meant he hadn't let himself get to know many women. He wondered if he should start with Nel. *That* was why he should be asking her to leave. Instead, he walked over to her, hammer in hand, and lifted the gloves off the mantel.

"When you fill up the box, let me know. I'll carry it out to the dumpster."

She looked at the gloves in his hand instead of at him. "Thanks, but I would've figured out a way to reach them eventually." She took them from him and wiggled them onto her fingers, still not looking at his face. "And I can carry the box out myself."

She lifted her chin, squared her shoulders, and turned her back on him. The picture of obstinacy and independence—an attractive combination if the quickening of his pulse was any indicator.

Grey headed back to his corner of the room, using the distance to cool his libido, reminding himself two months wasn't enough time to renovate a house *and* convince a stubborn woman to mess around with him. And that was a good thing.

If Nel let her guard down, he'd only end up pushing her away.

CHAPTER FOUR

They worked in relative silence for three whole hours, which was fine by Nel. She preferred the meditative quality of manual labor, over dealing with the unnamable vibe that came from Grey. Was it shyness? Stress? Anger? Maybe Rena was right about him struggling with his father's death. Being in this house, making these changes, maybe it was all too much for him. Maybe he did need a friend.

Nel wasn't his friend. She was his realtor, and she knew better than to get cozy with a client. It skewed the working relationship; made it harder to remain objective, which in turn made it harder to sell a house. She didn't need any more odds stacked against her when it came to selling this particular one.

Tossing the last box of broken tile into the dumpster, she headed back inside. Her stomach growled. A cheeseburger would be nice. And a beer. Something about pushing a broom and being covered in construction dust had her jonesing for bar food.

"Why are you so interested in this house?" He met her at the top of the stairs, a bottle of water inches from his lips. His words were curt and his eyes like slits. "There's got to be other houses you can list that need less work than this one."

Nel tried to tell herself that some people's curiosity was more aggressive than others, but his inquisition still startled her after hours of silence had lulled her into a false sense of security. He was a stranger with a gruff side, and now he'd turned that gruff side on her.

The impulse to fight back puffed her chest, and she forced an exhale to relax, which wasn't easy. Telling Grey she needed this house because she couldn't manage to claim a listing over the one-hundred-thousand-dollar mark wasn't going to reassure him she was the best person for the job.

"Why do you need to make a million dollars?" she asked, turning the heat on him instead.

The question seemed to startle him. He shifted his weight back, putting more space between them, and he dragged his fingers in a V-shape over his bearded chin.

He blinked, blinked again, and then shrugged. "I *want* to make a million dollars. That's all."

Nel nodded, only partially disappointed by his lack of meaningful answer. "Fair enough. I *want* to list this house. That's all, too."

His lips twitched, but then he walked away, into the kitchen, where he set the bottle on the counter and picked up his phone. "How long were you planning on staying?"

Awkward. He didn't call her an interloper, but his words sure made her feel like one. She walked deeper into the room until she could glimpse the great room, sans atrocious tile. Stripped down to the subfloor, it looked like a war zone instead of a million-dollar property. The irony of progress, and they still had so far to go.

She would stay until the job was done.

"I was hoping to start on the wallpaper tonight. My steamer's in the car." Nel nervously flicked her wrist over her shoulder in a mindless motion toward the front of the house. She half hoped he would kick her out so she could head home to a warm shower, but not before stopping off for that burger and beer.

"Then I'll order something to eat while we work. Got a preference?"

She smiled at the stroke of luck. "Actually, I do. A burger. I know this little place down the street. They don't deliver, but it won't take me more than ten minutes to pick it up."

"Fine," he said, nodding. "I'll pay."

She was stunned silent for a moment by the motion of him bending an arm to slip his wallet from the back pocket of his jeans. At some point during the floor demolition, he shed the long-sleeved flannel, leaving him clad in a simple black T-shirt that stretched across his chest, shoulders and biceps, but gathered loosely around his waist. She knew he was built. He was a professional athlete, for cripes' sake, but her brain knowing didn't translate to her heart keeping a steady beat.

He held out two twenties pinched between his thumb and index finger. She followed the thick chord of muscle in his forearm all the way up to the crook of his elbow before sanity kicked in and she waved him off.

"I'll pay," she said. "I can write it off as a business expense."

He narrowed those dark eyes, peeling away one twenty-dollar bill. "We'll go half."

That was reasonable. She always went halfsies on dates these days. It kept her in the clear, not owing the man anything. Not that this was a date. She simply didn't want to owe this man anything more than the million bucks she already promised… that was plenty.

"Fine," she said, taking his twenty. "But I get double American cheese, and they charge me an extra seventy-five cents, so it won't be exactly half."

He smirked. "Then order me double cheese, too."

Her stomach tumbled. She was hungry. Famished, really. But she knew the hollow in her belly had something to do with Grey, too. She just decided to ignore that little tidbit.

Once Nel ordered the food, they got back to work, scoring the wallpaper in preparation for steaming. Again they worked in silence. This time it bothered her more. At times he seemed receptive to conversation; she even saw a hint of dry humor now and then. But it was probably hard to maintain talkative and happy in his father's house, knowing his father was dead.

Maybe he needs to be consoled. Rena's voice nagged in Nel's head all the way to the pub and back again. If she were hurting, like Grey might be hurting, wouldn't she appreciate a sympathetic ear? Forcing a little more conversation as they shared a meal couldn't hurt.

Too bad she didn't know where to start.

Sitting in a heinous black lacquer dining chair Grey brought out from another room, Nel balanced a white foam container on her lap. She brought the burger to her lips and sucked in the chargrilled-scented goodness hanging in the air. She took a bite, savored the juicy flavor of meat drenched in cheese, and chewed longer than necessary, swallowing slowly, swallowing again even though nothing was there.

When she couldn't put off talking any longer, she cleared her throat. "Did you grow up here?"

He stared at his burger and frowned. "No. Milwaukee, Wisconsin."

That was it. He asked nothing of her in return. Simply bit into his burger and shut down her attempt at conversation. It didn't surprise her. He wasn't a man of many words, but oddly enough, the few he said encouraged her. At least he answered her question instead of telling her to go to hell.

She looked around the dusty, destroyed great room and figured she might already be there. If not for the delicious burger in her hands …

"Are you from Pittsburgh?"

The fact that he asked the question surprised her enough to make swallowing her last bite painful. Nel nodded and smiled past the burn in her throat. "Yep. I left for college but came back. That happens a lot around here. All four of my brothers moved away at different points, and all four ended up right back here."

He stared at her, the intensity causing her to squirm in the uncomfortable seat. She looked at her burger, studied the bite marks, and picked at a loose piece of lettuce—anything to settle the ridiculous nerves he stirred in her.

"Are you close with your brothers?" he asked.

"I am," she said, allowing herself a little relief that he was keeping the conversation going.

"Are your parents still married?"

"They are." She looked at him, because something about the question sounded off.

He wasn't looking at her. His head bent forward as he picked sesame seeds off the bun in the box on his lap. And then he stood, dropped the box of half eaten food on the kitchen island and walked away from her, back to the great room, where he switched on the steamer and went to work.

Oh well, at least she could tell Rena she tried.

•••

Lindsay's parents had been divorced, like Grey's. Her father remarried and had a second family Lindsay never got to know. Their resentment toward their parents and the siblings they saw as better off somehow bonded them during study hall senior year. Apparently it didn't bond them enough to keep her from cheating on him with his own damn father.

Grey held the steamer in one spot a little too long, allowing a backup of steam to scald his hand. He didn't even flinch. The anger bubbled, but he did his best to ignore it, peeling strands of slimy paper off the wall until his fingers cramped with pain.

Nel worked alongside of him, using a scraper to lift whatever remained. More than once he glanced over at her, catching a twisted expression on her pretty face. Had he put it there with his moodiness? Probably. A twinge of guilt mixed with his earlier anger, and the emotions hardened beneath his solar plexus, putting pressure on his lungs. He didn't ask her to go digging around in his past. Hell, he didn't ask her to be here.

Another blast of steam, and his fingers were burning again. This time a growl pushed past his lips, releasing some of the pressure inside. A man could only take so much, and honestly, he was damn near the end.

"Trade me," Nel said.

She was angled toward him, offering up the scraper.

"Why?"

"You're getting frustrated, and I don't blame you. This sucks." She lengthened the last word. "Wallpaper should be illegal. Maybe it will help if we switch every so often." She thrust the scraper toward him. "Come on; give it. We're wasting time."

There it was again. That thing about her—whatever it was—that made him want to let down his guard and let her in. Who knew he had a thing for bossy women? Not him. He only ever let himself have a thing for one woman, one woman who screwed him over and ended up dead before he ever got the chance to call her a bitch to her face.

"Never mind. If it means that much to you, steam your little heart out." She went back to scraping.

He was a complete tool. With a grunty sigh, he nudged her upper arm with his elbow. "Take it."

"Not if it's going to make you blow a gasket." She bit into her bottom lip, looking nervous.

He'd noticed that about her, too. Quick with the take-charge words, but a bit of worry while she waited to see how they'd be received.

Maybe he could try being normal for a change. "I'm not going to blow a gasket." Christ, if he hadn't already with everything he'd been through, he wasn't going to now—over a wallpaper steamer.

She wasn't convinced. A perfectly arched brown hitched while one side of her face scrunched comically. "You sure looked like you were."

"I was just…thinking. About something else."

"Yeah, well maybe you should try talking." Her eyes lifted over his face. "It's like a pressure cooker in there."

"Tell me about it."

"No." She put her hands to her hips. "You tell me about it, so we can move on and be productive. Two months isn't enough time under the best circumstances." Her expression softened, her lips parting. He wouldn't have been surprised to hear her sigh. "I'm sorry about your father—I am. I can only imagine how hard it is to be in this house without him. I'd be sad and angry, too, if my dad died."

Grey couldn't be that normal; he wasn't that normal. He felt the muscles in his face tighten and the blood rush to his head. "Yeah, well, I'm glad my dad died. He was a bastard."

The scraper fell from her hand, smacking the subfloor, while her brows rocketed to her hairline and her mouth formed a perfect O.

It was going to be damn near impossible to "move on and be productive" after that pronouncement.

"I don't know what to say." She found her voice much faster than he expected.

He shrugged and placed the steamer to the wall. "You don't have to say anything. We're supposed to be renovating a house, not spilling our guts." He hated spilling his guts.

"But…" In his peripheral vision, he saw her bend to pick up the scraper. "How can you drop a bomb like that and then not explain yourself?" she asked.

The scratching of the scraper against the wall mixed with the gurgling sound of the steamer. There were two things wrong with her question. One, it wasn't a bomb—not to Grey. He'd been living with the truth for so long now he was numb to his father's failings—at least he liked to think he was. And two, he didn't owe her an explanation. His life outside what he did to this house didn't concern her.

"So the money's some sort of retribution, isn't it? You want to make as much off him as possible, because you hated him." She was angled toward him again, lips twisted, skin bunching at the top of her nose.

You don't owe her anything, he reminded himself, and yet words formed in his head. What was the worst that would happen if he told her? She'd ask even more questions, and he'd have to relive every gory detail he'd been trying to block out. She'd also see him for who he really was—half a man, because only half a man could lose a woman to a man twice her age.

Nel waited, nostrils flaring. He didn't understand why she looked so pissed, unless having a normal, loving relationship with her father made her some sort of champion for dads everywhere. He wanted to tell her everything then. Letting her think he was half a man was better than letting her think he was the kind of man who unjustly hated his father.

Besides, it wasn't like nobody knew. Jordon knew. A few guys on the team knew. Of course, they took what little Grey gave them, and were satisfied with it. They didn't push for more, like he suspected Nel would do. Guys had about as much interest in knowing the ugly emotions of the events as Grey had in reliving them. Women were different; they liked to commiserate and help each other heal.

Grey just wanted to forget. And yet, he had a feeling his best shot at peace was to tell the story quickly, like yanking a bandage from a forearm scab.

He winced. "My girlfriend cheated on me with my father."

Again with the arched brows and O-shaped mouth. "No," she finally managed.

"Yes."

"I'm sorry." She set the scraper on the floor and flipped the switch on the steamer, plunging the room into deafening silence.

Grey tightened his grip on the steam plate until his fingers ached. "She was on the plane with him when it crashed."

"Oh my God." Nel slipped the ball cap from her head and squeezed her scalp, probably trying to let the ugly details work their way in.

Standing there, watching Nel process his words, he realized he'd never shared the story with a woman before—not even with his sister-in-law, despite her being a psychotherapist, despite Jordon's nagging him to sit down and talk to someone, like Maggie. Nel's reaction wasn't quite what he expected. She looked shocked, sure, but she didn't shower him with pity. At the moment, with her thin, pale hands wringing the hell out of her baseball cap, she seemed mad.

"Who does that?" she asked, contorting her face. "I mean, what kind of *father* does that?"

And then their eyes met, and she calmed down, slipping the hat back on her head without pulling the curls through the back. He liked her even better this way.

"I'm sorry." She shrugged. "I got carried away. You don't have to answer those questions."

"Okay." His lips hitched to one side.

"Good." She bent to pick up the scraper. "We have work to do."

When she straightened, she wrapped her free hand above his on the steamer plate, her smallest finger brushing his thumb. They were barely touching, but the skin-on-skin warmth had his body buzzing. He loosened his grip, allowing her to take the tool, but not before he hooked his thumb around her pinky in an odd sort of intimacy, one that caused her to freeze mid-motion. Their eyes met again, and his mouth went dry. He had the craziest urge to close his hand around hers, draw her in and wet his lips with a kiss.

"You really have a thing for this steamer, don't you?" A grin erased the wary sparks in her eyes.

This time, he let his lips curve completely. "Maybe I do."

He sure as hell wasn't talking about the steamer.

CHAPTER FIVE

Nel looked to her phone for the time, and then to Rena, who perched on the edge of her desk waiting for details about Nel's hours spent at the Kemmons house. Rena loved getting juicy details, but she was going to have to wait a while longer.

"I need to finish these contracts before the Smiths get here," Nel said, patting her palm atop the papers on her desk.

"You're trying to change the subject."

She was, but she wasn't going to admit it, because she didn't want Rena to know how confused Grey made her feel.

"I promise to give you details as soon as the Smiths sign on the dotted line and leave the parking lot."

Rena huffed and slid into her chair. "You're going to bore me with details about wall color and flooring, aren't you?"

"It's exciting, Re, watching this house come back from the bowels of hell," Nel said, a little heavy on the enthusiasm.

"Yeah, yeah. It'd be more exciting if the whole process involved a naked baseball player…or shirtless. Yeah, shirtless would do."

Nel rolled her eyes, trying to scatter mental images of Grey without a shirt; all lean athlete, the hard plains of his chest softened by a blanket of dark curls. Air fluttered in her throat, and she did her best to keep her breathing in check. Rena was a hawk, and if Nel's shoulders rose and fell too much, she'd swoop in for the kill.

"Tell me you don't think he's yummy," Rena added.

With her gaze glued to the contract in front of her, Nel lied, "I don't think he's yummy." She quickly followed the lie with a truth to calm her churning stomach. "I think he's complicated, scarred, and a bit unstable."

But the yummy part was getting harder to ignore. It changed complicated, scarred, and unstable to darkly handsome, tortured, and passionate—any number of words that dangerously romanticized the man's flaws.

Rena scoffed. "You're lying. Besides, even if he was all those things, who cares? He's around for two months—less than that now—and then he's all over the country playing baseball. No worries. If you keep it about sex, how complicated could it get?"

Nel should've known this would be the advice to come from a woman who had been having sex with the same man for four years—and she still refused to admit the man was more than a friend. From Rena's perspective, two months was still acquaintance territory, and the perfect amount of time to cut loose without relationship strings attached. But from Nel's perspective, two months was all it took for infatuation to render her stupid enough to let a man of questionable integrity mess with her head.

When Nel fell, she fell hard, opening herself up to being taken advantage of. She promised herself that what happened with Will would never happen with anyone, ever again. Business first. And when her business was thriving she'd have plenty of time to slowly, deliberately find someone to share her life with.

By then, Grey would be long gone.

"If we keep it about the house, it won't get complicated at all," Nel said. "That's the best approach."

"That's the boring approach."

The phone rang. "Saved by the bell," Rena teased.

Nel wished, but a phone call wasn't going to save her from the conflict brewing in her belly since spending the day with Grey. She could divide the hours into two groups: pre- and post-bombshell. She still couldn't believe his father slept with his girlfriend. As a screen junkie, Nel had witnessed a lot of dysfunction in movies and on TV, but what Grey's father did, seeing the pain of it in Grey's eyes, trumped the most twisted plot—and had Nel seeing Grey… differently. She hadn't completely changed her mind about him. No, it was more like she understood him, and she sympathized.

It sucked to be screwed by someone you loved. She had no idea what it felt like to have a father who was anything less than The World's Best Dad, but she had a lover who ended up the biggest, lying, cheat in her world.

Sure, Will hadn't been unfaithful in the classic sense, but in some ways what he did was worse. When he named a partner who wasn't her after all his heartfelt promises, he might as well have slept with his entire female office staff. Betrayal was betrayal, no matter how it was cut. So, yeah, she got Grey. And "getting Grey" had her mind wandering; her thoughts indulging. *That* had her worried. What if she did something stupid like focus more on getting to know the man than renovating the house? As it was, in the last sixteen hours, she'd thought more about his tragic story and surprisingly beautiful smile than she did about wall colors and hardwood flooring.

A smile, no matter how gut-wrenching, wouldn't make them a million bucks.

The longer Nel spent sweating in that house, the more she questioned her ability to command such a price. But after yesterday, she understood why he wanted the large sum…at least she thought she did. It probably was some sort of retribution, sort of like punitive damages for enduring what his father had done.

She wanted him to get every penny.

Despite the snarl of feelings and the nagging thought she should stay away from the house—and Grey—today, she planned to head over after work and tackle kitchen demolition. They'd be sledgehammering cabinetry and wielding power tools. They wouldn't be standing around chit-chatting, getting to know each other better.

There was nothing to worry about.

Riiiiiight. Nel blinked and the empty contract beneath her fisted hands came into view. She needed to focus on her workday. With a shake of her head she determined to do just that.

"Liar, liar, pants on fire," Rena said, laughing.

Nel had no idea how long Rena had been off the phone, apparently watching Nel struggle with her thoughts. She looked up to rebut or brush off the playground rhyme with a snide comment of her own, but Rena had spun the screen of her laptop around so it faced Nel, and all seventeen inches of LCD filled with a full-color picture of a beardless, baseball cap-wearing, grinning Grey.

Rena laughed harder. "Yum, yum, baby."

Staring at his smiling face, Nel couldn't find a single brain cell willing to argue.

So it was going to be that way. Fine. She was attracted to him, but just because she was didn't mean anything was going to happen.

• • •

Five hours later, creeping down Route 19, Nel gave herself props for managing to stop home to change and still make it to the Kemmons house with daylight to spare. Leaving the office early was one of the perks of being a business owner. And she was doing all of this—from grueling manual labor to unsettling interaction with Grey—for the sake of her business, she reminded herself.

Focus on the prize.

The real prize wasn't commission on a million-dollar home, although that was nice. No, the real prize was staking a claim on an upper-class neighborhood. A realtor's business thrived on referrals. Nel had seen entire neighborhoods claimed by one firm on the merits of one fast, lucrative sale. To stake her claim on

Mulberry Run and expand into the Glenridge neighborhood would change the demographics of her business, not to mention increase her income.

Something she thought about with a little less enthusiasm… staking a claim here would also put her head-to-head with Will Fortune, who'd been trying to weasel his way into the South Hills for two years now. But it was slow going for someone so entrenched in the northern suburbs. He'd been lucky a time or two, but nothing made enough of an impact to translate into a referral base that mattered. Heck, Nel hadn't seen a FOR SALE sign in these parts for at least a year; partially because people loved the neighborhood, and partially because listings stalled in the dead of winter.

But that was about to change, and Will wasn't going to like it.

Despite the shard of gloom that wedged between Nel's breasts whenever thoughts of Will came around, she smiled up at the Kemmons house, slowing the car's speed so she could appreciate the stunning Georgian-style mansion. All the physical labor and mental turmoil was going to be worth it in the end.

The garage doors were open.

Turning into the driveway, Nel glimpsed Grey standing in the middle of the three-car garage, staring at his feet. He had what appeared to be a broom handle shoved into a drain that was overflowing with black goo.

When she pulled into the drive, he looked up, a twisted expression on his face.

It *was* all going to worth it in the end, wasn't it?

She pushed out of the car, shoving her keys into her back jean pocket. "That doesn't look good."

His grimace tightened. "It's not," he said, looking down, drawing Nel's gaze along with him. Black sludge continued to bubble from the backed-up drain. "About that plumber…"

Nel slipped her phone from her front pocket and scrolled through her contacts. She wasn't happy about the setback, but she was happy she could further prove her worth to Grey—from a professional standpoint. She liked to earn her money.

"It's going to cost me an arm and a leg, isn't it?" Grey asked.

"Nah. I'm really close with the guy. He'll give you a good deal."

When her brother answered, she turned her back on Grey and walked down the driveway out of earshot.

. . .

She had a boyfriend. Of course she had a boyfriend. Whatever made him think she didn't? And why did it bother him so much?

Unbelievable. He jammed the end of the broom handle he was strangling into the drain, knowing full well it wouldn't do a damn thing to break the clog. Staring down sewage, and his biggest concern was Nel's relationship status? *Idiot.* All the construction dust must've coated his brain, making it too clogged to function. *Just like the fucking drain.* He stabbed it again.

"That's not going to help." She strolled up the driveway, lifting the bottom of her Pitt sweatshirt to slip her phone into her front pocket. Her jeans were tight, her stomach flat, and he glimpsed pale skin before she dropped the hem. His gut clenched. Now was not the time to be horny, and Nel was not the woman to be horny for. He would never make a move on a woman who was taken— he was not like his dad.

"I know it's not helping," he snapped, sucking too much ripe air into his nose and nearly gagging. "How long until your boyfriend gets here?" *Smooth; real smooth.*

She stopped, standing outside the garage, eyes wide. He wondered how much of his moodiness she'd take before she walked away. No commission could be worth dealing with him.

"He's not my boyfriend." Whether from his attitude or the smell in the garage, her nose wrinkled. "He's my brother."

Grey's grip loosened on the broom handle. He wished he wasn't so relieved. He also wished he never brought up the topic in the first place, because now he was dying to know if she had a boyfriend.

"I don't have a boyfriend," she said, seemingly reading his mind. And then she shot him a wrinkled-brow look full of attitude. "I'm sick and tired of stroking egos."

Despite the fact that he figured the stroking egos comment was directed at him, he felt a grin coming on. She was feisty and brave, and he liked it—he liked her.

So she didn't want to stroke his ego. Lucky for him, there were other things she could stroke.

His grin was cut short by a gurgling sound at his feet.

"I bet it's tree roots," she said, stepping closer, but standing outside the ring of black.

Her shoulders sagged as she shook her head. The gesture socked him in the gut, making him wince. "Brother or no brother, how much time and money is this going cost?"

"A lot." She nodded. "Best case scenario, Paul runs a cutter down the line and breaks up the roots, but you'll have to note it on the seller's disclosure, which could hurt us during negotiations."

Grey returned to strangling the broom handle, so hard now he was surprised the wood hadn't cracked. "And the worst case scenario?"

"The garage floor and driveway down to the curb gets jackhammered so the terracotta pipes can be replaced with PVC, and then new concrete will have to be poured when the job is done."

He closed his eyes and wished for a whiff of fresh cut outfield grass. Once again, he questioned why he was here and what he was hoping to prove. Wouldn't going to see his newborn nephew be a big enough gesture of brotherly love where Jordon was concerned? Maybe.

But Grey couldn't walk away now. He owned this godforsaken house with the master bedroom he couldn't enter for fear of getting physically ill, and the gutted kitchen, and the backed-up sewer, and …

The urge to throw the broom handle against the garage wall overtook him. He yanked the stick from the hole and opened his eyes, a muscle twitch away from launching the wood from his hand. But Nel was standing there.

"Why is it so important to you?" she asked, her voice not a whisper, but not the usual matter-of-fact tone he was used to, either. "Making a lot of money on this house isn't going to change what he did."

They were words he didn't want to hear. Flicking his wrist, he sent the broom handle skipping across the garage floor in the opposite direction of Nel.

"Maybe not. But he owes a million bucks to somebody important, and that's a debt I'm going to make sure he pays."

"Sounds like something you should let the police handle."

Grey scoffed. "It's too late for that." Stepping outside the mess on the garage floor, he walked to the lowest corner where he could breathe fresh air. He pressed his back to the cinderblock wall and drove a hand through his hair. "This is the only way to pay back my brother."

Once again he'd shocked her with something he said. She walked closer, brows arched high, shoulders rising and falling with each noisy breath.

"Your father owes your brother a million dollars?" she asked.

"Yep." And even though he didn't have to tell her more, for some reason he wanted to. "Years ago, he was Jordon's agent. He negotiated a million-dollar signing bonus, and took the money and ran."

More noisy breathing, and then silence as she gnawed her bottom lip.

"He wasn't a very nice man," she finally said.

"The worst." But he decided to keep the extent of it to himself.

"I'm sorry."

Grey nodded, sorry too, but unable to voice the sentiment past the thickening in his throat.

"What about your mother?"

The vacuum in his heart sucked free the blockage in his throat. "She died. A long time ago."

A harsh expletive slipped from Nel's pink lips, the ugly word so foreign coming from such a pretty woman, he almost smiled.

"I'm messed up," he said instead.

"Nah. All things considered, I think you're doing well." She stepped closer, sweeping a hand to her side, gesturing to the mess. "Dealing with all this for your brother's sake? When you could be…I don't know what baseball players do when they aren't playing baseball, but surely you could be doing something better than this. This is amazing."

It didn't feel amazing. Being here felt physically and mentally exhausting. Between the dogs and the memories, he wasn't sleeping through the night, despite sixteen-hour days spent wielding a sledgehammer and power tools. At this rate, he'd show up in Florida too tired to run down a shot to the wall.

Nel stood beside him, placing a hand on his sleeve. "We're going to fix this house, and then we're going to make a million bucks. I promise." She squeezed his arm and let loose a smile that pinked up her cheeks and shined in her clear blue eyes.

Now, that? That felt amazing. And he smoothed his hand on top of hers to tell her so.

CHAPTER SIX

Nel jumped when she heard a car engine, ripping her hand from underneath Grey's and spinning around to see Paul's van rolling up the driveway. She widened her guilty smile and waved frantically, a heavy thumping in her chest.

She was in big trouble…and it had nothing to do with the sewer.

"Hey," Paul called, as his work boots dropped to the cement.

"Hey," Nel called back, conscious of the slight quiver in her voice. Her face felt on fire. Her mouth was bone dry. And all her traitorous brain wanted was to turn back the clock to the moment when Grey's hand rested on hers, and she'd been lost in the magnetic pull of his gorgeous eyes.

Stupid.

Paul clomped past her, his tool belt weighed down with wrenches and a filthy flashlight. He was dirty, but he was always dirty. Even clean Paul looked gritty. Somehow all that grime didn't dull the shine of his great big heart. As far as brothers went, he was the best. When they were little, he'd been the only one to let her crawl into his bed during thunderstorms, and when she was a teen, and Johnny Krebs had called her flat-chested, Paul threw a punch to defend her honor. And here he was today, after hours, away from his wife, helping his little sister out again.

"Paul Parker." He held out a hand to Grey. "I hear you got tree roots."

"That's what Nel says." Grey glanced at her, making eye contact and Paul seemed to disappear.

She stood there, locked in unsettling, silent communication with Grey, but she had no idea what information was being exchanged.

Was he mad she suggested tree roots? Did he doubt the claim? But he didn't look upset. His eyes were soft; the skin around them smooth. And she had the deliciously unsettling feeling he was thinking about her in a most favorable way.

She looked away.

"Let me hook up my machine and see what we find." Paul headed back to his truck, leaving Nel and Grey in awkward silence.

She poked the toe of her tennis shoe into a crack in the cement and determined to keep things professional. After all, she had no proof it was anything but. Reassuring touches did not equal lustful moments.

As if to test the theory, she stole a glance at him. He stood with his hands on his hips, staring at the drain, while she stood at the edge of the garage, wringing her hands. He didn't seem to be showing signs of the unrest that plague her; probably because he wasn't thinking the same way about her. She wanted to believe it, but the air buzzed with something uncomfortable, something that pushed on Nel's chest, urging her to speak.

On the heel of those thoughts, what would she say?

"Paul's a good plumber." Not that. *Dork.* She wanted to slap herself in the forehead.

Grey didn't lift his head all the way, but he lifted enough to see her. His eyes crinkled at the edges. "Good to know."

"I just didn't want you thinking he's not as good as someone else, because he's my brother."

He stared at her a little too hard, a little too long. "Yeah, I wasn't thinking about your brother at all."

Her heart lodged in her throat, trapping a whimper. The intensity of his gaze heated her face all over again.

"Have you had trouble with the drains before?" Somehow Paul's question and the clanging of the machine he pushed up the driveway were louder than Nel's pounding heart.

This time she didn't jump or turn around. She simply stayed where she was and let Paul come between her and Grey. Nothing questionable could happen with Paul around.

"I don't know," Grey said, looking up to answer Paul's question. "I don't actually live here. I'm not sure how much Nel told you, but I just took on ownership of the house about a month ago. Looking at the way the rest of the house was cared for, I'd say the drain problem's not new."

Conversation flowed between the men, giving Nel a break from Grey's intense spotlight. Unfortunately, that didn't mean she stopped thinking about him.

She shouldn't have touched him. Touching him breeched the boundaries of professional and personal. And she definitely shouldn't have held his gaze when he looked at her like he wanted to dip his head and touch his lips to hers. She pinched the inside of her upper arm to stop from swooning. A physical relationship with Grey Kemmons was not what she wanted or needed. She didn't want any man right now. She wanted a successful real estate agency. And someday, when the agency was top of the heap, she'd make time for more than casual dating, get serious, find a gentle man, a sweetheart, who didn't mind if his career took a backseat to hers. Grey Kemmons was the direct antithesis of that man.

She tipped her head to the side so she could see around Paul's shoulders and stole a glimpse of Grey. Her heart fluttered. *Stupid, weak muscle.* There was no reason for it to act this way. Her head knew the score. She felt sorry for Grey; he'd been through a lot. End of story.

Grey laughed at something Paul said. It was no more than a chuckle really, one that bobbed his broad shoulders and nodded his head. She'd never seen him so unguarded. His wide smile looked unnaturally white surrounded by the black of his beard. He said something about centerfield, and laughed again.

The sound slid into her ears and down her neck, straight to her belly, leaving tingles in its wake. Her reaction to him didn't feel anything like pity. It felt like pure lust. Loud and clear.

When Paul's booming laugh filled the garage, she stole the chance to breathe deeper, scattering the tingles and slowing her heart rate. Then she slipped her phone out of her pocket in search of a way to stop obsessing about feelings she didn't want to be feeling.

The screen showed three missed calls from Rena. Nel would never understand how she failed to feel the phone vibrate when it was basically pressed against her skin. She sighed. No voicemails, so she clicked through to new text messages instead. All from Rena.

Hey.
Called u. Call back.
Hello?
Why aren't u answering me?
WHAT R U DOING?
?????????????????
Fine. I didn't want to do it this way but…
Fortune Agency has 353 Mulberry Run on MLS

Nel backed out of the garage amid the men talking and the clanging of Paul's machine. She looked up and over the Kemmons house until her gaze came to rest on the bronze address plaque. Three-fifty. Which meant three-fifty-three was …

She turned around in time to see the post digger pulling up in front of the Tudor house across the street.

It was happening again, wasn't it? Will Fortune was going to steamroll her.

• • •

"I like your brother." Grey shoved the iron bar beneath the kitchen tile and torqued the tool until the tile cracked. He liked Paul even more after he didn't find any tree roots and left him with a free-flowing drain.

"Everyone does."

He waited for Nel to elaborate, but like she'd been doing since Paul left, she kept it short and not-so-sweet. There was an uncharacteristic edge to her voice and an aggression in the way she worked. He blamed it on whatever happened between them in the garage. Obviously Nel wasn't enthusiastic about the spark between them—a first for him. Prompting enthusiasm from the opposite sex had never been a problem, even when he was with Lindsay. Not that he ever indulged. Unlike her, he believed in being faithful; it was a value he'd come by the hard way.

Shoving the iron bar beneath the next line of tile, Grey lifted with a grunt, sweat beading on his hairline and dripping to his temples. He crooked an arm and wiped at the moisture, reminding himself he'd been a stupid kid stuck between a lousy father he wanted to love and a big brother he barely knew. Now, Jordon had his respect and faithfulness. Thank God, he accepted it. Grey only hoped Jordon would accept the million bucks, too. Maybe then Grey would be absolved of the lingering guilt.

A bang vibrated the floor, shaking loose pieces of tile and mortar. Grey snapped his head in Nel's direction. She'd dropped a cabinet on her way to the door.

"Why don't you let me help you with that?"

She shook her head.

"At least let me break them up before you haul them out."

"No."

"Why?"

"Because I'm capable."

"Clearly."

She glared at him, hands on hips.

He didn't have a lot of experience with confrontational females. His mother had been a doormat and Lindsay kept the ugly parts hidden. But Nel, she put it out there, didn't she?

He might as well put it out there too. "You want me to apologize for making eyes at you in the garage? Fine, I'm sorry."

Her brows drew together. "I don't...I'm not..." and then she laughed, a tinny sound that confused the hell out of him, but still managed to make him smile, "...I forgot about that. And honestly, that's the least of my worries."

She forgot about it? The bruised ego made him wince. "Then what's the worst of your worries?"

"I don't want to talk about it."

Fine. He supposed; he didn't like when people tried to pull things from him.

"But I promise you it won't affect my abilities as your realtor," she continued. "I'm even more committed to selling this place fast and high."

"Even though the house across the street is now for sale?" He knew enough about supply and demand to know two houses for sale on the same block couldn't be optimal.

Those blue eyes widened, and she gasped. "I said I didn't want to talk about it." With a grunt, she hoisted the cabinet to her hip and shuffled away.

So she wasn't happy with the competition. She seemed so certain when she guaranteed him a million-dollar sale. Why did it feel like now her guarantee was conditional?

He didn't have an answer, so he worked the thoughts from his head until he realized she'd been gone longer than necessary to toss a cabinet into a dumpster. She'd been gone long enough for him to finish chipping up the kitchen floor; so long he figured it high time he went looking for her.

He found her sitting on his front stoop, staring at the house across the street. The pointed peaks of the brown and tan house shined in the glow of strategically positioned spotlights. He looked back at the dark shadows of his father's stone-cold house. Comparison-wise…well, there was no comparison. He bet the inside of the house across the street was as perfect as the outside.

The throbbing in his head intensified.

"Hey," he called to her when he was halfway up the cement walk. "Am I working you too hard?"

She shook her head and then dropped her face to her hands. Her elbows rested on her knees, and her rounded back expanded with each breath. He had the ridiculous urge to slip a hand beneath her curls to cup her neck.

But then she lifted her head for a noisy inhale, her exhale sending a puff of air from her mouth into the chilly night air. "I need to be straight with you."

"Okay." For some reason he felt like he should sit, but she was smack-dab in the middle of the stoop. He sat anyway, nudging her shoulder with his hip as he sank to the cold cement beside her.

She slid sideways, leaving a few inches between them. Funny, but as cold as it was all around them, the right side of his body— the side closest to her—stayed warm.

"I'm not sure I can sell this house for a million dollars," she said with a whimper. "And you have no idea how hard it is for me to admit that."

The light above the front door showered her in yellow, sparkling in her hair. Her face was shadowed, but he could see her drawing her bottom lip between her teeth. He should be concerned about her revelation. Instead, he wanted to flick a thumb across that lip and free it from the torture she was inflicting on it. Then, he wanted to turn her face to him and kiss away her worry.

He was officially crazy, wasn't he?

"My agency is small. What it lacks in size I swear to God I make up for in heart, but sometimes…sometimes that's not enough. Like when we're talking a million dollars and the house across the street just got listed by the top agency in the city." She looked at him, pulling her brows together, pursing her lips, and generally staring at him like he was a great buffoon. "Are you listening to me?"

"Not really," he said, offering a smile in his defense.

She huffed. "Why not?"

"Because all I can think about is doing this." He gripped her chin between his thumb and finger and tugged until his mouth met hers.

Her jaw tensed, and for a few long seconds, her lips didn't move. But then she exhaled, warming him with her breath and relaxing her mouth enough for him to slip inside. She tasted like she smelled. Black coffee with a hint of peppermint; and damned if his body didn't crave a double shot of caffeine.

He slid his hand to her neck, smoothing the curve of her jaw with his thumb as he deepened the kiss, exploring her mouth, stirring an overwhelming need. He wanted her, had to have her. Right here, right now.

She pressed palms against his chest, scorching his skin. But when she pushed again and her neck muscles clenched, it was like a bucket of cold water, dousing the flames.

He let her go, even though he didn't want to.

Prepared to apologize, Grey shifted his weight to put more space between them, hoping she wasn't too angry. Nothing about the kiss felt forced, but never again would he think he knew what a woman was feeling.

She blinked at him, her eyes a liquid blue in the porch light.

"Why'd you do that?" she asked, tracing her fingers over red and swollen lips.

There were lots of answers to choose from. He could play it smooth and self-assured with a '*because I wanted to.*' He could go with romantic, which for him usually meant something uncomfortable and cheesy, like '*because I can't get you out of my head.*' Or he could do what he did best, deflect.

He grinned. "I wanted to help you out." He hitched a thumb in the direction of the FOR SALE sign across the street.

"Now that's the least of your worries."

CHAPTER SEVEN

Nel didn't think it possible for things to get more awkward between her and Grey, but that kiss had gone and done the impossible.

She drifted around the empty kitchen, waiting for him to finish up with the dogs in the den. Every other minute, she convinced herself she should leave, and yet she was still here. Why?

She growled as she bent over to pick up a loose piece of tile and tossed it in a box. If she didn't think she had a shot in hell at selling this house for a million dollars, then why was she still here? Probably because she'd never liked backing down, especially when it had anything to do with Will Fortune.

Will's latest pretty young thing, Tawny Kellogg, was the listing agent for the house across the street. The home was impeccably decorated and high-end from floor to ceiling. Nel wanted to cry when she saw the virtual tour, and she wanted to puke when she saw the list price. Nine-seventy-five. What justification did she have for listing Grey's home higher? He kissed well? She held in a groan with a grimace, and tried not to indulge in any more thoughts about the kiss.

Apparently, she didn't try hard enough, because her very next thought was why he kissed her in the first place. Did he really like her? Or did he feel sorry for her, finding her sniveling on the stoop? Maybe he didn't like her-like her so much as he was curious. And maybe after they kissed, he wasn't curious anymore. Maybe he was disappointed and certain he didn't like her. That would explain why he didn't kiss her again.

Gah! Nel smacked her forehead, wishing she could scatter the thoughts, but they remained.

During the kiss, Grey didn't act like a disappointed man. He had acted like he wanted her, and he made her want him. Those feelings were unexpected and scary enough for her to push him away. Only now, she sort of wished she'd let the kiss run its course. Maybe then she wouldn't be obsessing.

Nel threaded fingers through her hair at the scalp, trailing down the strands, finding a chip of tile stuck in the curls. Seriously, why would he want her anyway? She flicked the chip to the dusty subfloor. He hadn't seen a single part of her that was attractive. He saw her pushy from the get-go, emotional on the front stoop, and dirty at all points in between.

She brushed the grime from her hands and onto the denim covering her thighs. None of that should matter anyway. Grey kissed her for whatever reason he had, and she ended the kiss because she was scared. The time to analyze this was on the stoop while they stared stupidly at each other until Grey invited her back inside…to work on the house.

The only thing that mattered was the house.

Regardless of what happened on the front stoop and regardless of what was happening across the street, their focus needed to be on the god-awful job they started.

Nel bent again, reaching for another broken tile, only to freeze at the sound of heavy footsteps. She wasn't ready to see him again. What would they talk about?

Not the kiss. Please, not the kiss.

"I'm starting to worry about the dogs."

She straightened, tossing the ceramic chunk into a box, thankful he wasn't talking about the kiss.

He poured himself a foam cup of coffee from the carafe she'd brought earlier in the day, and leaned against the wall, raising the cup to his lips.

Her brain stuttered, leaving her body without direction, leaving her eyes focused on his very capable mouth.

"I'm sure that's cold," she mumbled, telling herself it was noble to warn him.

Her gaze stayed on his mouth until he lowered the cup. Then she followed the sensual movement of his throat.

"It's fine," he said, smacking his lips, licking them, too, drawing her attention upward.

She blinked, tried to remember what he'd first said when he walked into the room. He said something before this inane conversation about coffee, didn't he?

Oh. "The dogs." She was thinking out loud, which, considering her Grey-centric thoughts, was dangerous.

"Yeah." He drank again, pushed off the wall with a bend of his elbow, and walked to her. "They spend a lot of time alone in that room or alone in the run. That can't be good."

He stopped in front of her, raising the cup to his lips.

Lord help her, she watched his mouth again, watched him swallow, told herself it was only because light lips circled in dark hair created such a contrast it acted like a target. But then her lips started to burn with the memory of being abraded by his kiss, and she couldn't deny the real reason for her fascination.

He stepped closer. "You should stop looking at me like that."

She stepped back, making sudden eye-contact with him. "Like what?"

"Like you want to crawl inside this cup so I can swallow you."

Liquid heat flooded her body, lubricating her joints, and buckling her knees. She opened her mouth to respond, closed it because she couldn't think of anything to say, and then opened it again, letting her ten-year-old self take control. "I did not do that."

"Oh, no?" He stepped closer. "My bad. Maybe you'd like me to crawl inside the cup so you can do the swallowing."

She squeaked, holding out a palm to stop his next step, only succeeding in firmly planting her hand on his rock-solid abdomen. Touching him had her anticipating all sorts of wicked things. The warm, wet pressure of his mouth; the erotic scratching of his beard…across her cheek, her throat, her breasts, her belly, her thighs…she shuddered.

"I haven't even touched you yet," he whispered.

"Maybe you shouldn't. I'm dirty."

"So am I." He grinned, offering up dusty palms as proof, and then sliding them over her sleeves to her shoulders, stopping when he cradled her neck.

Her throat heated at his touch, and she swallowed over and over again trying to douse the burn. But only one thing was going to put her out of her misery.

So she gave up, gave in, wound her arms around his neck and, pulling him closer, kissed him.

• • •

Grey hadn't expected to be kissing her again so soon after being pushed away on the front porch, but here she was, wrapped around his neck, pressed against his aching body. He wasn't going to complain about anything other than not being prepared to take this further. Of all the things he figured he'd need to renovate this house, condoms weren't included.

This was a dead-end kiss.

But Nel didn't know that. She wrapped her arms tighter, lapping at his lips, arching against his length, pushing her soft belly against his hard dick, and an irrational need to have her right there on the filthy kitchen floor roared through his veins. He dropped his hands from her neck to her hips, digging his fingers into the cushion of her curves, holding her to him, breathing heavy against her mouth, tasting her, feeling her, wanting her, knowing it was all going to end. Way. Too. Soon.

But not yet. He slipped his hands beneath her sweatshirt, cupping the warm skin at her waist, sliding his palms up her rib cage, riding the gentle waves until his fingertips brushed the band of her bra. His skin tightened, a ball of nerves sticking in his chest. Adrenaline, like before every game; how he loved the rush.

He held the soft, warm weight of both covered breasts in his hands while her rapid breathing fluttered against his wet lips. He was hard, hot, and frustrated, but he pushed on, freeing her breasts from their silky prison, holding her bare in his hands. It was torture, knowing he'd have to stop soon.

He brushed his thumbs across her nipples, and she whimpered against his mouth, pulling harder on his neck. He buckled under the weight of everything.

And then she reached for his zipper, smoothing a palm to his crotch.

He stepped back. The kiss broken. The moment shattered.

"I can't." His breathless words echoed.

"Oh." She was a glorious mess of wide-eyed, blushing need, and he hated himself for not being able to satisfy her.

"No condom."

"Ah." She nodded, even managed to smile.

It was more pleasantry than she'd get from him. Grey couldn't do anything but stare at her for fear he'd do something stupid, like drag her off to one of the spare bedrooms despite the missing equipment.

"Another time," he finally said.

She nodded again, the blush fading, and he couldn't help but feel stupid, like a bumbling teen, who missed his only shot.

"I should go…it's late."

He nodded. "Yep. We can finish tomorrow."

He glanced at the mess they'd made of the kitchen, but he knew his comment had more to do with finishing what started between them.

She didn't acknowledge either task. She simply adjusted her bra and tugged on the hem of her sweatshirt as she crossed the great room. He followed, picking up his pace so he could pass her and open the front door. When she brushed by him and out into the cold, she did so with barely a glance.

"Bye," she called, flipping her wrist, a move that looked half wave, half brush-off.

He couldn't shake the feeling he wasn't going to see her again.

•••

Nel didn't get much sleep. She tossed and turned, dodging thoughts of Grey. Wanting him…not wanting him. Wondering where either decision left his house? He needed her. And no, not *that* way…although he had made it pretty clear he needed her that way, too. So intense. If needy could be sexy, then Grey cornered the market, making her underused libido scream, "yes, please," while her overprotective heart yelled, "hell, no."

In the end, she didn't trust herself to make the right decision.

So when Paul called the office shortly after noon to ask if the drain remained clear, Nel saw an opportunity to make it all a little easier. She didn't have the right to ask her brother for another favor, but she asked anyway, knowing it wouldn't make Grey happy. She asked because it would make her feel…safer. To her surprise, Paul agreed to help with more than the plumbing in the kitchen at the Kemmons house. Bringing in Paul on the job was the right thing to do.

With three people doing the work, the house would be finished faster than expected, and Nel could list it and get on with her life, one that focused on real estate market domination, not adolescent boy-girl histrionics.

After Paul's call, she worked more efficiently, content she'd be safe from making a stupid carnal mistake where Grey was concerned, but underneath it all was dull worry she was doing something wrong, something backhanded that would hurt more than help.

Grrr! Why couldn't Grey be old or ugly—or female? Biology would screw everything up if she let it. But she wouldn't, because a little sex wasn't worth a lot of messy feelings clouding business decisions. Being screwed by Will—both ways—taught her that.

When she thought about Will, she didn't like to think about the good parts, about the beginning, when they'd met in real estate licensing school. He came to every class in a suit with the swagger of a successful property investor. Being from a working class family, Nel had never known a man like him. And when he sat in the seat beside her, night after night, filling her with the scent of his expensive cologne, he made her swoon.

Five years later, when Will told her he'd named John Evans agency partner, he made her scream. Literally. And she made a scene in the office they built together. He said he was only thinking of her—of them—of their future children. Didn't she want to have kids and stay home to raise them? A lighter work load was supposed to make it easier for her to walk away.

She walked away, that was for sure. Business and pleasure didn't mix.

Which was why she needed Paul to run interference with Grey. She couldn't afford to be rationalizing lusty feelings for a client.

"We need a new copy machine." Rena charged into the main room and slapped a pile of papers on Nel's desk. "There's a thin blue line through everything. It's decapitating you on these brochures."

It was an ironic representation of Nel's ability to lose her head around Grey. She grimaced and nodded. A new color printer wouldn't come cheap. A sixty-thousand dollar commission—thirty if she had to share with the buyer's agent—would certainly help.

"While you're at it, we could use a new coffee maker. Ours sucks. It's so slow, and I'm not running vinegar through it again. The coffee's starting to taste like salad dressing."

Rena was in quite the mood, but Nel didn't complain. With Rena spouting off about shoddy copiers and inefficient coffee makers, she was too busy to be asking questions about what was going on with Grey. Which was great news, considering what *was* going on with Grey.

Still, Rena's moodiness left Nel wondering, *what gives?* And as her best friend, she could only ignore it for so long.

"Is everything okay?" Nel asked.

"No," Rena huffed. "Haven't you been listening to me?"

"I'm listening, but I'm not convinced your mood is because of faulty office equipment."

"Whatever." She spun around and raced to her desk, where she picked up the telephone receiver, hung it up again, shuffled some papers, and then roared. "Ben asked me to move in with him. He said he's ready to take the relationship to the next level. And I was like, 'what relationship?'" She tossed her hands into the air. "Living together? I'm not ready for that."

Which wasn't surprising. Nel had never even heard Rena refer to Ben as her boyfriend. Considering the ambiguous state of the relationship, moving in together seemed premature. And yet they'd been sleeping together for four years. Friends with frequent benefits—something Nel couldn't understand.

"Ben's a great guy," she said, wanting to help Rena, but knowing it was complicated.

"I know."

"Then what's the problem with having a real, romantic relationship with him?"

"What if he's not the right guy? What I commit, move in with him, and the next day I meet somebody who sweeps me off my feet and makes me lose my mind?"

Grey. Nel closed her eyes amid a fresh flush of memories from the night before. She chased them away with a clearing of her throat. "Just because a guy does all that doesn't make him the right guy."

And who was Nel trying to convince? Certainly not herself. There was no reason to think Grey was the right guy for anything Nel had planned. Even if he wasn't just a blip on the radar screen of her life, he'd still be nothing like the man who would someday be right for her.

Nel sighed.

Rena sighed, too. "I don't know what to do. I can't make up my mind, and Ben keeps calling and texting. He wants to go to dinner tonight. I'm so worried I'm going to say something just for the sake of saying something, and I'm going to regret it the rest of my life."

Nel could relate. There was something daunting about being alone with a man who wanted something you weren't sure you should give.

"Come with me tonight," she blurted. "Help us out with the house. Paul's going to be there, too. It'll keep you busy."

Us busy.

Too busy to make stupid mistakes.

CHAPTER EIGHT

Grey unloaded boxes of hardwood flooring off the bed of his pickup truck. With help from his beard and the bill paid in cash, he managed to make it out of Lowe's without being recognized. He even slipped into Wal-Mart next door, and with his head down, used the self-checkout to purchase some things. It dawned on him during the drive back to the house that maybe nobody would've paid a lick of attention to him either way…but he wasn't taking any chances.

All it took was one baseball fan calling into one talk radio show, and everybody would be wondering why Nashville's Gold Glove winner was in Pittsburgh. There'd be speculation about a trade, and before long he'd be the talk of *SportsCenter*.

Even worse, if it became public knowledge that he was buying condoms in a suburban Wal-Mart after the untimely death of his girlfriend, there'd be enough drama attached to the story to put Grey on *TMZ*'s front page.

Under the best circumstances he wasn't comfortable with notoriety, and attracting attention now would only screw things up; tipping off Jordon about the house and robbing Grey of the element of surprise. If Jordon caught wind of this project, he'd argue, and there was no doubt he'd refuse the money if he knew how much work it was going to take. For things to go as smoothly as possible, it was important for Grey to lay low.

At least he had the dogs to keep him company. And Nel.

He hoped he had Nel, but after the way last night ended he wasn't so sure.

He hoisted another box onto his shoulder and headed for the house, stopping at the sound of a car pulling up behind him.

She came back.

Relief flooded his body, and his muscles unclenched. He hadn't realized he'd been so tense.

Last night, while he laid in bed, sandwiched between two big dogs, wishing he was sharing mattress space with Nel, he asked, *why her, why now?* A million thoughts pinged back and forth in his head, but he kept honing in on one simple truth. Having her around made him feel better—almost normal—and it'd been a long time since he felt like that.

He turned, eager to see her expression, hoping to see her smiling face. But she wasn't smiling, and she wasn't alone; it wasn't even her car.

Paul popped out of the driver's side of his van. "Hey, man."

"Hey." Grey lifted his chin as further acknowledgement. *Why are you here,* weighed heavy on his tongue, but he bit down, holding it in.

Grey liked Paul and Paul's inappropriate humor. Grey laughed more while working on the drain yesterday than he had since the season ended. He missed the guys, and having Paul around sort of filled that niche. But having Paul around also changed the dynamic of things. Spending hours alone with Nel was something Grey looked forward to.

"Surprise." She hopped down from the passenger's seat, slamming the door behind her. "Paul agreed to help us out, and we brought my friend, Rena. You remember me mentioning her, right? Well, she was free tonight, so I thought why not? They're sworn to secrecy—right, guys? And with four of us, we can bust this reno out in no time."

Grey didn't bother acknowledging the woman who emerged from the van next. He was too stricken by a nervous Nel. She was babbling, not making eye contact with him, and it was so different from the meeting he'd hoped for. The skin on his forehead tightened as he tried to process the turn of events.

Suddenly, the reason for Nel's entourage was crystal clear. She said Paul and Rena were here to "bust out this reno." In other words, she wanted to hurry up the job and get the hell out—far away from him.

Grey's gut clenched in an I-told-you-so move. He'd been right to worry about the way she'd left last night. She'd been all business the day they'd met; apparently the breech in professionalism made her retreat.

A voice that appeared when Lindsay left, a voice he hated, sneered. *She doesn't want you as much as you want her.*

The story of his fucking life.

"Good," he growled, feeling his muscles harden again. "You can unload the truck while I check on the dogs."

He stalked inside, dropping the box of hardwood planks to the subfloor in the great room. The contents made an awful racket, but he didn't care if he scratched or cracked a board. Nel and her "work crew" could take care of it.

His old friend Anger slithered free of its cage and walked side-by-side with him through the house to the back hall. Grey clenched and unclenched his hands, breathing in and out through his mouth, trying to reset his brain, telling himself he didn't need Nel.

He could have any number of women in the world. He was a professional athlete. It was part of the game—getting laid was a given. All he'd have to do was shave off the beard and head to a bar downtown. One word about his profession and he'd have a harem of half-drunk females at his disposal.

The idea didn't sound appealing.

He'd picked up women a few times before, after Lindsay ran off with Dad. But it wasn't all it was cracked up to be. It felt a lot like being given the night off, sitting your ass in the dugout while you watched the goddamn game. Yeah, sure, you were there. Same sights and sounds, but you were missing something—something big.

He winced, remembering those mostly silent, too-damn sweaty, uncomfortable encounters. Not one of those women came close to lighting him up like Nel did.

The thought prompted a growl.

Stalking down the hallway, Grey was back to wondering why she mattered. Worse yet, why didn't she want to have sex with him? He ought to be thinking, *fine, good, I don't need the trouble anyway*. But he wasn't. His ego wasn't pleased; his ego demanded he prove her self-control wrong by showing her again exactly what she was missing.

He knew he was a moody bastard, but he didn't think he was that much of a jerk. She was entitled to her decision. He thought about throwing a fist against the wall, but then he thought better of it, shoving hands into his jean pocket instead. If only she hadn't felt so damn good in his arms, then he could move on without another thought about her. What was wrong with liking someone, feeling something, and wanting to act on it? Nothing more, nothing less.

Nel was making it too complicated. At least her brain was making it too complicated, because as far as he could tell, her body was an eager participant. She didn't want to stop last night any more than he did. He tasted the desire on her lips and watched it sparkle in her eyes. And come on! The second time *she* kissed *him*.

Grey had to find a way to remind her of that—despite the people she'd brought to run interference.

Unbelievably so, by the time he reached the door to the den, he was smiling, certain Nel wanted him, but she was playing some sort of game. He wondered how long it would take for her to realize she didn't have a chance at winning.

After all, she was up against a man who got paid to play.

The more he thought about it, the more he liked the idea. After all, he'd been working a lot lately…too much maybe. Now, it was time to have a little fun.

•••

Nel banged the mallet on the edge of the hardwood, locking the plank into place. She glanced up to thank Paul for the freshly cut pieces he stacked by her feet, and then she looked over at Rena, who was standing with a paintbrush in one hand and her cell phone in the other.

"I thought the purpose of tonight was to keep you away from all that," Nel said, walloping another board with the mallet, frustrated for too many reasons to explain.

Rena stuck out her tongue. "And I thought the purpose of tonight was *helping* a client, not doing all the work for him."

What could Nel say? Rena was right, though Grey disappearing to play with the dogs wasn't unusual. He did so off and on whenever Nel was here. But to do it precisely now; to be gone for forty-five minutes when they'd just arrived to help? That seemed rude, even for Grey.

She smacked another plank and as the vibration bit into her hand, she admitted his rudeness was probably because of her. He didn't look happy to see her in the driveway. The few words he managed didn't sound happy, either. Could she blame him? He had no reason to suspect she was bringing reinforcements, not after last night, not after what happened between them. There was an insinuation they'd pick up where they'd left off. With the renovation…and the sex. She could claim all she wanted that she brought Paul and Rena along to help with the construction, but it was mostly to help keep her feet on the ground instead of her back on a mattress. Her reasoning was starting to feel more than a little bit pathetic, especially in the face of Grey's negative reaction.

Still, he didn't know she brought Paul and Rena to interfere with whatever might have happened tonight. How could he? There wasn't enough interaction in the driveway for her to give herself away, and he didn't know her well enough to be predicting her behavior. Only a paranoid person would automatically assume she brought Paul and Rena to put a permanent wedge between them.

Nel closed her eyes on a sigh. What was she doing? This was Grey she was talking about. Of course he was paranoid. He had more reason than anyone she'd ever met to make assumptions based on mistrusting people.

Crap. She screwed up. She wimped out. She should've been straight with him in the first place. This was not the way Nel Parker did business. Standing, she brushed her hands clean and took a deep breath of dusty air. "I'll take care of it."

Her stupidity and his obstinacy weren't going to put this project at risk. Regardless of the real reason she brought Paul and Rena, with two extra pairs of hands they had a real shot at pulling off some stunning renovations. She and Grey just needed to pull their heads out of their asses long enough to get over what happened in the garage and on the stoop and in the kitchen…and focus on work.

Talking to Grey was the right thing to do. Even so, Nel walked softly down the hall, trying not to make a noise, giving herself the option to turn around if she wanted to. Every door but one was open, and from behind the dark wood, she could hear his deep voice mixing with yips and growls. She put her hand on the knob but paused for a fortifying breath. That's when she heard laughter. The sound warmed her, made her smile, made her think he was a good man who'd been mistreated by people he loved.

Nel shouldn't be adding to his trust issues by shutting him out. The thought was ambiguous, so she clarified…quickly. She needed to stop shutting him out of decisions about the renovation; she should've asked him about bringing Paul and Rena.

Shutting him out personally was a different story. There simply wasn't a big enough payoff to justify what almost happened last night. Orgasms were a dime a dozen and easy to achieve alone. There was something depressing about that thought, so she tried again. He was leaving…soon. And she had a job to do. She didn't need more of a reason to keep things professional than that.

Several breaths later, Nel didn't knock. She didn't want to tip off the dogs to her arrival and give them time to escape. Instead, she turned the knob and slipped inside the room, leaving the occupants momentarily stunned. But the minute her presence registered, Blackjack and Joker pounced on her, paws to her belly and hips, tongues lapping the air inches from her face. She couldn't help but give in to their incessant excitement, hunching over so they could lick her face.

Wrapped around them, she glanced deeper into the room, finding Grey watching her from his lazy position on a yellow leather sofa. He slouched in his seat, denim-covered knees resting wide apart. One arm dressed in faithful flannel stretched along the back of the couch. The other hand rested at his side: pure unadulterated male. And somehow she had the feeling he'd been waiting for her. That feeling buzzed in her chest, making it hard to breathe, making it impossible to remember why she was here alone with him in the first place.

He whistled. Not a friendly sound, a piercing call that had the dogs clamoring back to his feet. Even though she saw the love he had for them, the control he exhibited over them was unnerving… so was the ensuing quiet.

She straightened, smoothing her sweatshirt and finding her voice. "Paul and Rena were wondering where you were."

"*They* were?" His voice was low and rough. He didn't so much as blink.

More quiet lingered between them, but it wasn't awkward so much as it was unnerving. Nel focused on the dogs' gentle breathing instead…until she couldn't stand it anymore.

"I was wondering, too, but I know how you get wrapped up with the dogs when you're spending time with them, so I figured that was what you were doing." *Keep going,* she told herself when she paused for a breath and faltered. "I started laying hardwoods, but then I thought some more, and I thought you were probably in here because you're mad." She swallowed. "At me."

He blinked. Twice. And then he lifted the hand from his side to his chin, massaging fingers against his beard. The motion loosened a smile, a slow, lazy smile that had her blood buzzing and her body backing toward the door.

"I'm not mad at you," he said.

"You're not?"

"Nope."

"Good."

"Yep."

"Okay." She nodded, completely confused by what was going on. He just kept sitting there, smiling, like he expected her to rush across the room and leap into his lap.

Her muscles twitched as if it was the best idea her brain had all night. *Crap.* "I'll see you out there when you're finished in here." She turned and grabbed the knob.

"Nel?"

She didn't want to, but she paused, glancing over her shoulder. "Yeah?"

His smile grew bigger and tinged with something predatory. "Just for the record, I'd like to point out that even with your bodyguards, I managed to get you alone, didn't I?"

A spark consumed her from the inside out, until she had no choice but to breathe through open mouth, hoping to cool the flame.

"I don't know what you mean," she lied, knowing she shouldn't wait for him to answer. She needed to get out of this secluded room and back into the open where she was safe.

But his bright smile held her in place, like a deer in the magical glow of headlights. She sensed the danger, but she couldn't move.

"It's going to happen, Nel," he said, leaning forward, dropping his long arms to either side of his legs, rubbing the dogs behind the ears. He kept his lazy gaze on her. "One of these days. You and me. It *will* happen."

She blinked, and the mindless motion broke his spell. "But not today," she called as she yanked open the door and scrabbled from the room.

All the way down the hall, her heart slammed against her ribs, and her brain taunted her. *What a stupid comeback. That's the dumbest thing you've ever said.*

She couldn't argue.

Nothing like making herself a challenge…nothing like being turned on by the whole ridiculous game.

CHAPTER NINE

The earth tilted.

That was the only way Nel could explain what had happened, how she started the evening so sure of herself, and three hours later was second-guessing every move.

She expected to walk into the den and apologize to Grey for bringing Paul and Rena without telling him first. Then, she expected to walk out of the den with a clear conscience and a renewed vigor for the work.

Not for Grey.

A shaky breath passed between her lips. She couldn't take much more of this. Her knees ached from crawling around on the hardwood floors, her hand burned from wielding the mallet, and her head hurt from the racket of the circular saw. But none of that compared to the torture of working side-by-side with Grey.

How did she manage for hours upon hours before?

She wondered if there was a full moon. She never paid attention to things like that, but something was different. Something was making her more aware of him. Every breath she took brought the scent of him into her mouth, where it reminded her of how he tasted. Twice, she looked at him, wanting to tell him to give her space, but he unleashed a smile that chased her words away. And now he wanted her help, carrying boxes of flooring scraps to the garage.

She bet he did—anything to get her alone.

Nel tipped her head to her shoulder to stop the tingles left over from his whispered invitation. She had already said *no* once, but she didn't put it past him to ask her again.

"I gotta go," Rena said.

The sudden announcement startled Nel, who looked up to find Rena holding her phone, casting wide, begging eyes at the occupants of the room.

"Why? What's wrong?" A thick panic brewed in Nel's belly.

"Nothing. I just…" She crinkled her face, and behind the rapid blinking, Nel could see tears. "I need to see Ben."

It figured. While Nel was struggling, wallowing in confusion brought on by a man, Rena was struck with clarity about hers.

"Paul, I hate to ask this, but could you run me home?" Rena was pretty much begging.

Paul looked at Nel, and then back to Rena with a why-not shrug. "Sure."

Of course he'd say sure. He was a nice guy. Nel wanted him to be a nice guy; she just wished he could be a nice guy, staying right here in this room.

Nel watched helplessly as Paul pulled keys from his back pocket. She had a decision to make. Stay and finish the floor, risking alone time with Grey—which didn't seem smart—or call it a night and leave the mess to him, which didn't seem fair.

Rena lived ten minutes away, tops. Paul would be back. How much trouble could Nel and Grey get into with ten measly minutes and half a great room floor to finish?

The panic from her belly surged into her throat as Rena passed, following Paul to the door.

"I'm so sorry," she offered to Nel. "But I know what I have to do now."

Nel could only nod. If she said anything, she worried she'd beg Rena to stay.

"I'll be back," Paul called.

"No rush," Grey countered.

Shit. Nel closed her eyes and told herself to breathe.

A rush of cold air chilled her back, and then the door clicked as it closed, leaving her alone. With Grey.

She opened her eyes and stared at the floor, trying to anticipate his next move. Would he say something, pick up where he left off teasing her in the den? Or would he skip the words, invade her space, and make his prediction come true.

You and me. It will happen.

Oh, God, she was one sick lady, because she wanted it to happen, even while she fought it with everything she had.

"How 'bout some water?" he asked, his boots tapping against the new hardwood floors.

He was walking away, walking toward the kitchen, and her reply stuck in her dry throat. Water would be nice—great, actually—but she couldn't speak. Maybe she was in shock. She'd been so sure he'd pounce the minute Paul and Rena left.

She didn't know what to make of that, so she simply stared, bleary-eyed, at the dividing line between the finished and unfinished floor.

Even without her answer, he returned with two bottles in hand. She saw his boots in her peripheral vision.

He came into clearer view when he squatted in front of her. "Here," he said, offering a bottle.

Nel accepted with only a millisecond of eye contact and barely a brush of skin. "Thanks." At least that's what she tried to say. She wasn't sure the word was recognizable to him.

He drank while she took an overdramatic interest in the floor beside and behind her, inspecting every crack and crevice that wasn't around him. She had no idea what came next.

"Look at me, Nel." His voice coated her like body butter, thick and smooth.

Her brain said no, but she couldn't quite rationalize the slight, so she looked. And when she did, he smiled.

"I like the floors," he said. "You were right about the darker stain. I gotta give you props." He raised a fist, exposing his knuckles to her.

Fist bump? He wanted to *fist bump?*

She nodded, twisting the cap off her bottle, and then she guzzled until the plastic crackled in her hand and the bottle was empty.

Somehow the rush of cool water renewed her sensibilities, and on the heels of her lips smacking and the bottle hitting the floor, words rushed out. "I don't get you. All your talk in the den about getting me alone." She threw up her empty hand and pointed around the room. "We're alone, and all you want to do is talk about hardwood floors and fist bumping. I don't get that."

He arched his brows, the smile falling from one side of his lips. "Are you disappointed?"

She rolled her eyes, and her stomach followed. "No." She was only bringing it up to clear the air. Really.

Her brain seemed so sure, but her body buzzed with denial.

Seconds ticked by with him staring at her, and then he leaned closer…closer still. Until his breath blanketed her face. Until his lips brushed the hair at her temple.

She closed her eyes and soaked the sensations in. He was barely there, but he was everywhere. And she was freefalling, her stomach tumbling, her skin prickling with adrenaline. His lips grazed her cheek bone, inching closer and closer to her lips.

And suddenly her brain was onboard with her body. She wanted this. She wanted him. Reason and rationale be damned. The revelation relaxed her, and she readied for his kiss.

The kiss never came.

Seconds later, Nel opened her eyes to find him returned to his original position, squatting before her.

"Now are you disappointed?" he asked breathlessly, his eyes heavy-lidded and black as night.

This back and forth was going to kill them both.

Game over.

"Yes, I'm disappointed," Nel said, rolling up on her knees and sliding her hands over his chest to his shoulders. "So I'm going to change that."

Grey's arms wound around her waist and pulled her forward. When their lips met, their bodies tumbled to the floor. She sprawled on top of him, her hands cradling his cheeks, his hands cupping her ass, and there was no place she'd rather be than in his arms.

Fighting that didn't make sense.

• • •

Nel's resolve was easier to crack than Grey expected. Thank God, because restraining himself had never been his strong suit. Now he was certain she wanted him every bit as much as he wanted her, and knowing that was a beautiful thing.

With her weight distributed over the core of his body and her tongue sliding into his mouth, he gave into the vicious need, floating in a nameless, timeless space.

"Some idiot nearly…"

Paul's words morphed with the opening and closing of the front door.

A cold blast of air let in by his arrival blanketed the silent room as Nel scrambled to her feet, leaving Grey guilty as hell on the great room floor.

"Okay then." But by the set of Paul's jaw, Grey could tell nothing was okay.

"Hey. Paul. Did you get Re home? Was she quiet on the way?" Nel touched fingertips to her lips, and Grey saw her hand shaking.

He also saw Paul's right fist opening and closing as it hung at his side. From watching the guy work, Grey knew he was right-handed. He also had strength like an ox. Fortunately, Paul was a good foot shorter than Grey.

Grey stood. In situations like this, it was best to have every advantage.

"Let's go," Paul finally said. His words were even, but the fist still pumped at his side.

"But we aren't done," Nel said.

Grey totally questioned the wisdom behind her statement, considering the tension in the room. "We can be done," he said.

Paul glanced at him and gave a tight nod. "Listen to the man. He says you're done."

It was sort of comical, and strangely touching in a very foreign way. Grey liked Paul looking out for Nel. Growing up, Grey had only ever witnessed men treat women the opposite.

"Are we done?" Nel asked, looking at Grey. Her face was still flushed, and her eyes were sparkling.

She took his breath away.

He nodded. "For now."

"Okay." Her sigh echoed through the empty room.

"Thanks for the help tonight, Paul," Grey said.

Paul grunted. "I'll be back tomorrow. With Nel."

So the bodyguard would remain.

Looked like time alone with Nel was about to become a luxury.

• • •

Nel slammed the van door and let loose a scream. "What was that?"

Paul snorted. "My question exactly."

"Well, for starters, it was none of your business."

"You made it my business when you asked me to come along tonight."

True. But she had changed her mind, and she didn't need his protection. "Paul, you don't have a say in the matter."

"It's a free country, Nel. I can say whatever I want about the matter. And the more I think about it, the more I think Dad would like to hear about it and have his say, too."

"You wouldn't."

"I would."

Silence filled the front end of the van. Nel sucked the air filled with the smell of filth and metal tools, trying to calm her lust-turned-anger. She had asked for this, hadn't she? All because she couldn't face her desire for Grey in the first place. Paul was only doing what she'd brought Paul along to do.

"He's a good guy," she said in Grey's defense.

"Maybe, but he's also a professional athlete." Paul tossed her one of his big-brother-knows-best looks. "I didn't realize you aspired to be a notch on anyone's headboard."

Nel punched him—hard—in the upper arm. She didn't care if he was driving. He was being a dick.

"I worry," he said, groaning and rubbing his arm. "Guys are pigs. They're out for one thing—believe me."

He sounded so much like Dad.

Nel's anger softened. "Paul, I know how guys can be. You're forgetting I'm a woman with lots of firsthand experience with pigs. Well, one pig in particular."

"Exactly. Which is why I don't think you should be falling for the flashy guy again."

Flashy? It was a hardly a word she'd use to describe Grey. She knew Paul was talking about the baseball career, the house, and the money, but Nel didn't see Grey that way.

She reached across the space between them and rubbed the spot on Paul's arm where her fist landed. "I'm sorry for hitting you." He nodded. "And I promise I'll be okay."

"I know you will." He sniffed and puffed out his chest. "Tomorrow night I'm bringing Joe, Rick, and Greg."

Great. He wanted to make it a family affair. Nel chased away a fresh burst of anger with a hearty exhale, reminding herself once again she opened this can of worms by asking Paul to help in the first place.

"That's not necessary," she said. "Besides, Grey would never agree."

Paul leveled her with stone-cold eyes. "Then make him agree. Otherwise, I'm having a little chat with Dad."

Well, crap. Just when Nel thought she'd made up her mind and had things under control, the earth tilted again.

CHAPTER TEN

Grey bit into an apple. While he chewed, he admired the gleaming hardwoods and freshly painted walls.

Nel had been right about taking a classic approach. It didn't even look like the same house. And thanks to Paul, the fireplace looked fit for an English king, not fit for a disco queen. Progress; real progress. Grey could only imagine what it would look like by the end of the month—nothing like his father's house. Each crack of the sledgehammer, each push of the broom further erased the mark of Francis Kemmons.

Grey took another bite of the apple, savoring the crisp, bitter taste. Long after he swallowed, a sweetness remained on his tongue. He decided it was satisfaction.

Everything was falling into place. Including Nel.

He smiled and tossed the apple core into a contractor bag hanging from the knob on the basement door. He still wasn't happy about Paul tagging along to guard his little sister, but there were ways around that.

Slipping his phone from the pocket of his best blue jeans, Grey called up Nel's contact information. He'd texted with her a few times before about supplies and work times, but he'd never given her a ring. Until now.

He tapped *send* and put the phone to his ear, his blood buzzing with anticipation.

"Hello?" She sounded far away and hesitant.

"I want to see you." He cut straight to the chase.

"Hold on a minute, please." Noises muffled on Nel's end, and then she whispered, "You'll see me tonight."

"With your bodyguard," he complained, but the smile on his face kept his voice even.

"Try four."

Four bodyguards? Grey's smile flipped upside down.

"My brothers," she continued. "Paul thinks I need the help."

"You mean the protection."

"Yeah. They mean well."

Oddly enough, Grey knew they did. And once again he was filled with the same confusing mix of entertainment and satisfaction at her brothers' care of her. No, he wasn't pleased three more strangers would be lurking around his house, but right now he had a different focus.

"Meet me for lunch," he said.

"I don't usually take a lunch."

"Take one today."

"Why?" He heard a smile in her voice.

"You don't want me to answer that."

"I don't?"

"Nope, because if I do, you'll be so turned on you won't be able to work." He chuckled. "On second thought, maybe I will answer that, and you can cut out early."

"I'll see you at noon." Her breathy voice wasn't helping to quell his anticipation.

"I'll be waiting."

It was the longest two hours of Grey's life. He played with the dogs, straightened the guestroom he'd been calling his own, and then paced the floors for a good half hour, looking out the window in five-minute intervals. When he saw her car in the driveway, his stomach ended up in his throat.

He was always a ball of nerves before a big game.

She stepped out of her car, and he was pushed back in time to the day they met, when she was wearing a suit and an all-business expression. He hadn't seen her in anything but sweatshirt and jeans since.

His brain registered a knee-length skirt, showing off shapely legs and bad-girl shiny black heels. Lust dislodged the ball of nerves in his throat, and he groaned. He wasn't sure he was man enough to handle her, but he was damn sure going to find out.

Again he waited, but this time was even more painful, because he could watch while he waited, watch her hips swing as she walked, watch her loose curls swirl in the breeze. Every muscle in his body hardened, preparing for action.

Before she even reached the front stoop, he was sweating. Not giving her the chance to knock, he opened the front door and with an arm to her waist, dragged her inside.

"Hey," she sort of squealed, slamming against his chest, sending a puff of soft perfume in his direction. "Down, boy."

"Not a chance," he growled against her lips.

He heard the thud of her purse hitting the floor, and felt her arms wrap round his neck, and then her mouth opened over his and their tongues entwined, satisfying the ache that had been growing inside of him since last night had been cut short.

There'd be no interruptions now.

The next thing Grey knew they were standing in the middle of the guest room, sucking the air out of each other, his hands shoved inside her suit coat, her hands under his T-shirt, clawing at his back. He didn't like the rampant pace. So much of his life seemed beyond his control and worthy of forgetting, but not this.

He loosened his grip around her waist, dragged his mouth from hers and breathed. "Are you in a hurry?" he asked, moving on to nibble her ear.

"Are you?"

"I don't want to be." He looked at her then, her mouth swollen and irritated from the friction of his face, and for the first time since the season ended, he wished he didn't have the beard. He smoothed the splotches with gentle swipes of his thumbs. "Unless you have an incredibly short lunch hour and an obligation on the other end."

"I told Rena I had to meet a guy about a color copier and I didn't know how long I'd be." Her tongue darted out to taste his thumb when he brushed across her bottom lip. "I have time."

"Then let's slow this thing down," he said, smiling, taking her by the hand and leading her to the bed.

Grey sat on the edge of the mattress and pulled Nel to him until she was lodged between his open thighs; her standing, him sitting. Eye to eye.

It took a couple breaths before Grey moved again, unbuttoning the two silver tabs holding her suit coat together. Everything about him was slow and precise, everything except his thrashing heart. With a flick of his fingers, the suit coat slipped from her arms.

Grey palmed her belly and breasts covered by a crisp white blouse, and the reverence of the motion took his desire from fierce to irrational. He touched her everywhere, over the top of her clothes, smoothing hands down her arms and along the bumps of her back, riding the curves of her ass draped in wool, slipping lower until he reached the bare skin behind her knees, her calves.

With his face pressed against her belly, his every breath was her; a soft sunny scent like a Gulf Coast afternoon. Damn if it didn't make him hungry for more of her.

He licked at the fabric of her shirt, sucking her belly gently while his palms and fingers memorized every slope of her calves. Lower and lower until he slid massive hands around her ankles, swallowing the small bones whole.

The pressure inside of him built, and he questioned the wisdom of moving this slow. That was when he realized her fingers tightened in his hair, and her rapid breathing filled the room. *What the hell was happening here?*

He straightened, feeling drugged, and he didn't have time to process anything more than Nel's kiss. She gripped the back of his head, forcing their mouths together in the hardest, hottest kiss he'd ever been part of.

And then she cut it off, sliding her hands to his cheeks, holding him still. "Let's speed it up a bit, shall we?" She added a grin as she darted her hands down his back, yanking his T-shirt over his head. Her gaze rolled downward, and her eyebrows arched. "*Mmm, mmm, mmm.* You sure don't disappoint a girl."

She reached out, tracing a finger along the center line of his chest, and his skin burned.

"I thought we were speeding things up?"

She laughed, slipped hands behind her, and the skirt fell to the floor. "Like that?"

"Like that."

Then she set fingers to the pearl buttons on her blouse.

Grey was mesmerized by the motion, the sureness in her steps as she walked out of her skirt and opened her blouse. With sunlight streaming in from an uncovered window and a devilish grin on her gorgeous face, she tugged on her collar, and then rolled back her shoulders, letting the blouse slide down her arms, but catching it with her hands. He stared at a simple, unadorned bra and panties a shade darker than the cream of her skin, and it became the sexiest lingerie he'd ever seen. Probably because she stood before him in nothing but that lingerie and heels.

The pressure peaked, making his skin itch and his eyes burn. He was seconds away from reaching out and pulling her in, but she caught him off-guard with palms to his chest and a shove that sent him falling to the mattress.

He thanked his lucky stars when she crawled over him. Because, hell yeah, he had a thing for pushy women. He just didn't know it until he met Nel.

• • •

Nel planted her lips to Grey's lips and sprawled over him, picking up where they'd left off last night on the great room floor. She liked this position, liked the way he groped her butt while his body heated her from beneath.

Of course, today was a little different from last night. There was less clothing. She ran her hands across his hard, wide shoulders and rode the curves of his muscular upper arms, all the while kissing him slowly, swallowing his every breath.

She still couldn't believe she was doing this, but it was too late to argue.

Warm hands slid beneath her underwear, holding her tighter against his solid body. She dropped her lips to his chin and his throat, as he slid his hands over her back, leaving tingles in his wake, tingles that melted inhibition and hesitation into wicked desire, pooling it at her core.

This needed to go somewhere—fast. Pushing palms to the mattress, she lifted so she could kiss her way down his chest.

He unhooked her bra, the wisp of fabric slipping down her arms, landing on his stomach. She maneuvered out of it, tossing it aside while he took her breasts in his hands and thumbed her already hardened nipples. She bit her lip and groaned.

Even with the push to speed things up, it was painstakingly slow. All of it. And something about the speed smacked of an emotional stickiness that was confusing as hell. But now was not the time to wonder about it. Her brain cells weren't exactly operating at full capacity. So she stopped thinking, sitting to straddle his thighs, feeling the burn in her groin from his body's width. But the burn was overshadowed by the slivers of pleasure he coaxed from her breasts.

She reached for the button on his jeans, and then his zipper. "We should have done this while you were standing up," she said with a shaky, gratified sigh.

A second later she was breathless and on her back, with Grey on all fours above her. He devoured her with kisses, while their hands battled each other to free him from his pants. And then he was naked, with her hands on his hard, bare hips, and he was tugging at her underwear, lifting her with his strength.

The panties made it as far as her knees before she wiggled out from under him and kicked them aside, all while somehow maintaining lip contact.

"I want top," she said in between kisses.

"I won't argue." And he was on his back again, pulling her over him.

In all her years, she'd never…Her over-stimulated brain didn't try to complete the thought.

Reaching between them, Nel took him in her hand, milking him slowly, listening to his breathing hitch. She let the lustful control whip her insides into a desirous frenzy, and when he slipped a finger between her folds and stroked her, too, she nearly broke. Gasping for air, rocking her hips, every inch of her burned with outrageous need.

"Condom," she rasped.

He dropped a hand from her hip and slid it beneath a pillow, retrieving a blue packet that he brought straight to his teeth.

Pure animal. The thought brought her to the edge, and she gasped again, grabbed the packet from his lips and took charge. She rolled the condom into place, while ogling the magnificent man who was at her mercy. Did he know she was at his, too?

She opened her mouth and drew a breath as he gripped her hips and slid inside of her.

Heaven.
Perfection.
Meant to be.

The list involuntarily lengthened as she moved above him, his fingers strumming the same slow, steady pulse on the hot, wet flesh between her overstretched legs. It didn't seem fair, that a man who made her feel like this would be here and gone, and there wasn't a damn thing she could—or should—do about it.

"You better plan to take a lunch break for as long as I'm here," he said, his voice rumbling.

She would've laughed if she wasn't already moaning in anticipation of the perfect orgasm.

He slid a palm along her side to her breast. One hand up, one hand down. Three more breaths, and the combination of sensations dumped her over the edge, filling her with wave after wave of euphoria.

When he tumbled, too, pulling her closer, burying his face in the crook of her neck, she didn't know what hit her.

But she knew one thing…she'd never look at her lunch hour as a waste of sixty minutes again.

• • •

Six hours later, Nel tried to hide her smile from Paul as they pulled into Grey's driveway. She didn't want her brothers to know she'd been here already today. What she did on her lunch break was none of their business anyway.

Joe's mini-van pulled alongside Paul's work van, and the rest of her brothers piled out.

Grey had no idea what he was in for. Thankfully, he was too sated to argue when she'd brought it up while they were still in bed. They really did need the extra help.

Paul pushed out of the van, meeting Rick and Greg in between the vehicles. Nel stared, shaking her head at the motley group. Now that she had the intimate logistics all straightened out with Grey, she wanted to be happy her brothers were here. This was the crew of workers she tried to suggest in the first place. Between the four of them, they'd rehabbed a dozen houses since Nel opened her agency. And the beauty about it was they accepted payment in beer.

Of course, she didn't get to tell Grey any of that before he shut her down, proclaiming no crew. Funny how things changed—even when you didn't want them to.

Joe motioned for her to get out of the van, so she did, bringing along with her an excitement to see Grey again, enthusiasm for the work they were about to do, and a touch of anxiousness over everyone getting along.

She was about to read them the riot act when she rounded the front of the van and came face-to-face with Rick and a case of beer. "What's that for?" Suspicion scrunched her face.

He looked at the rest of the Parker men, exchanging conspiratorial glances before he looked back at her and smiled. "You know we always share a few brewskies after work."

The others nodded and laughed.

She'd known them all her life, and she knew when they were up to no good. "I don't know what you're up to, but you guys better behave tonight. You're only here because I want you to be here. We've got work to do."

"Oh, we'll behave," Paul said with a slap to Joe's back. "We're just going to make sure he behaves, too."

CHAPTER ELEVEN

"Five guys in this room and there's not one stud?"

Grey stood back and watched four sets of eyes narrow on Nel.

"In the wall. For the cabinet," she stammered, and then slapped Rick's upper arm. "Touchy, touchy."

She was smiling, which was good and bad. Good because she must not be thinking things were going poorly. Bad because when that smile lit up her face all Grey could think about was getting her naked.

"Romeo, eyes over here," Greg said, looking at Grey from overtop a mahogany cabinet. "You've got a few inches on Paul. You wanna hoist?"

Romeo. Cute. Grey chuckled.

It took less than an hour working side-by-side for Grey to decide he liked these guys. He liked the way they didn't pull punches and badgered the hell out of one another—and him, too. It made him feel like part of something again.

"Sure," Grey said, switching positions with Paul, who seemed none-too-pleased to be replaced.

"Don't pout, princess," Greg teased. "You just forgot to wear your shoe lifts is all. Next time." He grunted and counted to three.

Grey tamped down a laugh with exertion. So far today he'd had sex, laughed, and got one hell of an aerobic workout in. It'd been a damn perfect day. Now, if he could just figure out a way to get Nel to spend the night.

Three hours later, the kitchen had come together, but Grey's plans for the evening fell apart.

"He'll take another. Give him another." Joe sipped his own beer while Rick passed a full bottle to Grey.

Grey didn't want it. Just like he didn't want the first two, but he didn't know how to say no, considering the work these guys did and the reason he wanted them gone. He could hardly say, "Leave, so I can have sex with your sister."

He took a hearty swing to wash down the tawdry thought. They were getting along, especially while basking in the satisfaction of a job well done and drowning in the warm flow of beer. But he knew it would change if he made an overly aggressive move toward Nel. So he let her come and go from the room, despite his desire to hunt her down and corner her and …

Grey wiped sweat off his brow with the back of his hand and took another drink. For a guy who didn't want any beer, it was sure going down easy.

"You think maybe you guys will agree to terms with Manion?"

It was the first time any of them had broached the baseball topic since Paul railed him in the garage about the time Grey face-planted the outfield wall against Pittsburgh last season. Paul waltzing up and breaking the ice like that was classic, and Grey appreciated the laugh. But right now, two-and-a-half beers in, he didn't want to be gossiping about his teammates.

He shrugged. "That's a question for Casey, not me."

There was relative silence from the men scattered around his kitchen, leaning on freshly mounted cabinets. A few smacks of lips around bottles, but nothing else until Nel waltzed into the room with a shredded towel in one hand.

"Those dogs sure take their tug of war serious." She flashed Grey a smile and brushed past him to the garbage bag.

Just the smell of her had him setting the beer on the floor while his back straightened. Full alert. There had to be some way to get her alone.

"Do I need to go back there and settle them down?" he asked, knowing he didn't, knowing it was a long shot.

She stilled alongside the garbage bag. "Ah, maybe. There might be…"

"Beer pong," Joe wailed from the open space opposite the kitchen island, where he was trying to bounce a wadded ball of masking tape into a coffee-stained white foam cup. "Come on. Who's first?"

Every one of them looked at Grey.

"Wait a minute." Nel charged into the center of the circle of men. "You're trying to get him drunk, aren't you?" She spun around with finger pointed like the spinner on a board game.

Nobody said a word.

A smile crept across Grey's face. They were trying to get him drunk. They were. And it was a brilliant plan. A drunk man passed out—he didn't have sex.

"We're done here. Let's go. Move it out." She was literally shooing them. "You guys think you're so smart, but you're not. Not at all. I could totally get in my car after you drop me off and drive right back over here."

She paused for a noisy inhale and a growl, and then she scrambled around the kitchen picking up empty bottles and tossing them into the trash bag. "I should've known. Look at this." She wiggled a bottle in the air. "We've been sitting here for how long and Greg's only finished half a beer. Ridiculous."

Silence.

Grey watched the guys accept their chastisement with stiff upper lips and downward cast eyes. He felt the tug again, the odd sense of sentimentality that overcame him when Nel and Paul were around.

She stopped in front of him, all five feet and change, chin lifted, shoulders back, and eyes like a gas-powered flame. He blinked and her lips were crushing his, her arms thrown round his neck, her body weight bending him at the waist. He didn't dare open his mouth to deepen the kiss or raise his arms to hold her. He wanted to. God, he did. But any minute now, four sets of fists were going to take him down.

"There," she said, swatting his chest as she released him, turning to face the other gaping men. "And for the record, I'm the one taking advantage of him."

Six weeks having a disadvantage to Nel? Grey could live with that.

• • •

After Nel's performance in Grey's kitchen, her brothers backed off, agreeing to stay out of her personal life as long as they didn't have to see anything else that made them twitchy. And to her surprise, the agreement stuck.

For the next three weeks she settled into a new daily routine, mornings at the office, private lunches with Grey—*ahem*—and evenings working on the house with some combination of her brothers. The progress was astounding.

But more than the house was changing. For the first time in ages, Nel was—more often than not—able to say *Will who?* without flinching when someone brought up Fortune. At first, she thought it was because all the physical exertion in and out of bed kept her too tired to worry about her next run-in with Will, but it was more than that. Even when she tried to play devil's advocate and conjure his image to test herself, the emotion wasn't there. Progress.

Enough so, she agreed to accept—in person—the award for Pittsburgh Real Estate's Female Mover and Shaker. She wasn't too fond of the title, but she wouldn't turn down an award attached to publicity, even if it meant coming face-to-face with Will, who was up for the big one: Broker of the Year.

Okay, Will being named Broker of the Year—again? *That* bothered her, no matter how much progress she made, but she wasn't going to let bitterness put a damper on the fun she'd been having lately. If she wanted to discourage happiness, all she had to do was count the days until Grey pulled out of Pittsburgh.

Nel frowned, but reminded herself he wasn't gone yet. She stuffed the melancholy deep in her belly with help from a blueberry muffin and tried not to think about Grey leaving. It wasn't even worth thinking about seriously until he was down to a week left— maybe even a few days. Rena said that tactic made Nel an ostrich. Funny how a few weeks of successful co-habitation made Rena an expert on relationships.

Not.

Nel wasn't buying it. She also wasn't buying Grey being anything more than her rebound from Will—despite the fact she'd broken up with Will a long time ago. There wasn't a statute of limitations on something like that, was there?

It wasn't even a relationship. They weren't dating. They never left the house, and that house was the reason they were together. Take the house out of the equation and there'd be no "them," no commonalities, no proximity—just a temporary need to sell a house in which they used their spare time to fill with sex.

Nel huffed, pushed her laptop aside and stared at the ceiling. Maybe she was lying to herself and Grey meant more than she cared to admit. The beauty of it was she didn't have to admit anything. Nobody was holding her under dripping water. And it wasn't like she had to worry about him reciprocating anything more than sex, so she could keep the mushy crap to herself. Caging her emotions was something she'd gotten good at after Will.

When she didn't flinch after thinking about him, she smiled. If the only thing that came out of her association with Grey was an indifference to Will, then she'd take it…with both hands.

Bolstered, Nel decided these "lunches" with Grey needed to be on her terms, and maybe today she'd skip altogether. Just to prove she could. She was a strong, independent woman who didn't need a man.

Her phone buzzed against the pile of papers stacked on her right.

Grey: Don't forget the whipped cream.

Her skin tingled; her mouth watered. How could she let him down by not showing up?

She could compromise, prove to herself she didn't have to rush over there and yet not leave him holding the can, so to speak. She'd go late and cut out early. It would be a weaning of sorts.

She had to start someplace.

• • •

Grey tossed a pile of his father's clothes onto the bed in the master bedroom and went in search of a box big enough to hold the designer duds. Somebody at Goodwill was going to get lucky. He smiled, actually smiled, at something related to his father. It still blew his mind he could walk into the bedroom his father shared with Lindsay and not want to tear things apart. He just didn't seem to care about them anymore.

What he did care about was whether or not Nel would remember the whipped cream she'd promised to bring. He looked at his phone again, anticipating her answer to his reminder text.

Nothing.

She was busy, probably with a client. Although if she was, she was going to be late for him. Grimacing, he looked as his phone again and reminded himself he'd see her soon.

Not soon enough.

The things he planned to do to her—with and without whipped cream. He chuckled. She'd been the best part of his day for the last two weeks. Heck, she was the best thing that happened to him since he arrived in Pittsburgh. And if he was honest with himself, she was the best thing that happened to him—outside of baseball—all year. Grey didn't like putting so much pressure on a person. People usually let him down. But it felt different with Nel somehow.

He snatched a box from the pile Nel assembled with castoffs from a grocery store and headed back down the hall. The doorbell stopped him. She was right on time. His grin stretched ear to ear.

But when Grey opened the door, it wasn't Nel. A tall, cool glass of water with long black hair and witchy green eyes flashed him a ruby-red-lipped smile.

"Hi, I'm Tawny Kellogg, the listing agent for the house across the street." She thrust a bony hand toward him. Her sparkly fingernails looked long and sharp enough to draw blood.

Two seconds after she introduced herself, Grey couldn't even remember her name. As far as he was concerned, she was Lindsay 2.0.

He shoved his hands in his jean pockets. "Did you need something?"

She blinked—a lot. Her eyelashes fluttered, and her smile widened. "Well, as a matter of fact, I've been in and out of the neighborhood for a while now, and I couldn't help but notice the dumpster. Are you preparing to sell, Mr…?" She arched skinny black brows as though she expected him to offer his name.

Grey was beyond meeting people's expectations. "I'm just doing some work for the new owners." It wasn't exactly a lie.

"Oh, so the house sold already?"

"The house changed hands."

"I see." She swayed to one side, flashing her eyes to the space behind him.

Grey straightened, swaying a tad, too, hoping to block her view. "If you'll excuse me, I have work to do."

"Of course." She blinked up at him, and her tongue darted out to kiss the center of her top lip. "God," she breathed. "I'd do anything for a tour. I'm a great lover of strong, sturdy… architecture."

He bet she was. Too bad for her, Grey had never been an eager tour guide.

"I can tell you right now the owner wouldn't be comfortable with that."

The owner also wasn't comfortable with Nel showing up while Lindsay 2.0 was here. If he didn't do something quick, everything would blow up in his face.

•••

Nel braked as soon as the house came into view. A woman stood on the front porch, garnering an audience from Grey. Her stomach bottomed out. A short wrap coat hid the woman's attire, but from the miles of visible legs Nel knew she was either wearing a short dress or a mini-skirt—and ridiculously high heels.

The FOR SALE sign across the street swung in the breeze. *Tawny Kellogg*. Only Will's agents dressed themselves like high-class call girls.

Why was Tawny there?

Ice filled Nel's veins. Maybe they knew about the house getting ready for listing. Fury lifted her foot off the pedal, and for a split second she aimed to floor the gas and take out Miss Kellogg right there in the grass. But Nel blowing her cover wasn't going to help things. She needed to trust Grey. He didn't want anyone to know the details of his project anyway, so let Tawny try.

Nel edged the car to the side of the road and meant to relax, but the conversation on the front porch stretched out longer than she expected, with Tawny tossing her head back and her black hair waving in the wind.

Nel's hands death gripped the steering wheel. What the hell? Why wasn't Grey getting rid of her? He knew Nel was on her way. Heck, she was late. Wasn't he worried?

Nel leaned closer, trying to get a better read on Grey, but he was too far away for her to see his expression. Her hands tightened further, and her jaw followed suit. She wanted Tawny to go. Better yet, she wanted Tawny to pull a neck muscle the next time she tossed back her head. Nel snarled—the woman was infringing on her territory.

If she could've, she would've kicked herself for playing games and coming late. If she'd been here—she glanced at the whipped cream can poking out of her purse—Grey would've been too busy to answer the door.

Why is she still there? Nel growled. He couldn't possibly be falling for anything that woman said. Nel hated to admit it, but her jealousy meter was through the car roof. This was Nel's time. That was Nel's listing. And Grey was Nel's man.

She dropped her forehead to the steering wheel and sighed.

Two out of three wasn't bad.

CHAPTER TWELVE

Five minutes ago, Grey was worried the agent-turned-flirt wouldn't leave. Now he was worried Nel wouldn't come.

He called her again, unsure of whether or not he should be worried—in three weeks, she'd never been late for a lunch date. What if she got in a wreck?

His foul mood, brought on by that ridiculous woman's inquisition, multiplied. At least Tawny was gone, and not lurking across the street. He looked out the front window to where her black BMW had been parked, and wondered how many more unannounced visits he was going to have to put up with. She didn't seem to understand the word *no*.

He sneered and roughed up the hair on his face. The closer he got to spring training, the more he thought about shaving off the beard, but he was glad he hadn't pulled the trigger yet. Was it possible she recognized him? Sure, it was. That would explain the surplus of flirting. Then again, maybe she really was just interested in this house. The structure had the same effect on Nel.

He looked down at his phone and frowned. Still no text or call from her. Before he could do something about his building worry, he looked up and out the window, finding something infinitely better than a text.

Nel's car was in his driveway. *Finally.*

Grey pushed out the door and took a big breath of crisp, cool afternoon air. He met her halfway down the front walk, anxious to get his day back on track. But she looked…off. No smile. No words to explain her late arrival. Her face was blank.

Dread slowed his steps.

As she approached, he saw the red cap from a can of whipped cream stuck out of her purse, and the sight reassured him. Not that this… whatever this was…was all about sex. These past few weeks, while she'd been ridding him of his clothes, she'd also—somehow—rid him of his resistance to relationships enough to have him thinking of ways they maybe could make this work. He supposed great sex helped boost the appeal of keeping her part of his life, but it was more than sex—it was her. The way she looked at him, talked to him, made him talk to her. It was like she held the key to opening him up and pulling all the ugliness out, and he didn't want to go back to before that.

"Are you okay?" he asked, reaching for her arm.

She nodded, pulled away and glanced over her shoulder. "Don't."

Damn. "You saw her, didn't you?"

There was enough distance between them for another person, and she seemed to want more, walking with one foot on the concrete and the other on the grass, despite her high heels.

"What did she want?" Nel's words were forced, clipped. They sounded nothing like her. Not even when she was annoyed by her brothers, or stressed by the amount of work they faced in a limited timeframe did she sound so agitated.

He needed to pick his words carefully, but he didn't want to lie to her. First of all, what did he have to lie about? He'd done nothing wrong. He hadn't sought out that woman, and he did his damnedest to get rid of her. But telling Nel the woman was sniffing around the house—and him—wasn't going to help Nel's mood. For a split second, he entertained the idea of not telling her everything, but her wide, clear eyes stared back at him like a mirror to his soul, and he knew she deserved the truth.

Grey sucked in some air and blasted it out his mouth, ready for things to get worse before they got better. "She wanted to list the house."

"And?"

"And I think she was looking to…you know…get with me."

Nel's blue eyes turned glacial. She tucked her chin in like she'd been sucker-punched, and though he didn't know exactly what he'd said wrong, he knew it was something big. He regretted his haphazard collection of words more than any other words he'd ever said—and he'd said some doozies.

"I was asking about the house. Tawny wanted to list the house, and I was asking what you said to *that*. She works for the most successful agency in town. They can be…persuasive. You and I don't have a contract. You're free to go with whomever you'd like."

"We're talking about the house, aren't we?" He honestly wasn't sure. The words seemed directed at their business agreement, but her eyes locked onto him like they did sometimes during sex, wide and magnetic, and he felt a connection that could bring him to his knees.

"I don't care about the rest," she said, snapping the connection.

Could've fooled him. She sure as hell looked like she cared. Granted, he didn't have the sharpest instincts when it came to women. But it was hard to miss how she stumbled over those words and attacked her bottom lip with her teeth when she'd finished speaking. Maybe she was just worried about the house. As if he'd consider listing with someone else. After everything she'd done for him.

"This is your house, Nel." He closed the gap between them and let his palms ride the curves of her shoulders. "I'd never do that to you."

She broke eye contact, inhaled and exhaled. "Thank you."

Something still wasn't right. Despite the influx of air, her muscles bunched beneath his hands. He rubbed, pulling his fingers over the knots at the base of her neck. This was not how he wanted to spend what little time they had together.

Grey lowered his lips to her temple, certain he could chase the tension away. "I see you brought me whipped cream," he whispered into her ear.

"Yep." But there wasn't an ounce of give in her body.

This was going to take some work.

• • •

Nel wanted to give in. She wanted to quiet her mind, relax her muscles, and follow him to bed. But she didn't. Everything locked tight, from her jaw to her toes to the tips of her heels. And she knew why. She didn't feel like having sex because she was feeling too much like a jealous girlfriend.

Which was not cool. It made her weak, and it undermined her business judgment.

"You want to talk about it?" he asked, still doing his best to massage the stress from her neck.

It was working—sort of. The heat and pressure from his palms felt good. It started the relaxation process, but then she thought of Tawny on the front porch wanting to *get with him*, and the tension built into a nagging headache.

"No, I don't want to talk about it." Nel was already idiot enough for feeling like this. She wasn't going to broadcast her stupidity.

His fingers walked up her neck, gathering at the base of her skull where they circled, circled, circled…Her head tipped to one side. She meant to blink, but her eyes closed, and they couldn't manage to open again.

Nel had no idea how long she stood there, limp and at his mercy before he said, "You know, you made me talk when I didn't want to."

"That was different." Her words were barely a whisper as she tipped her head to the other side.

"Doesn't seem different. You wanted me to talk because my mood was getting in the way. Seems like the same thing to me."

Was it? Maybe. She couldn't think straight anymore. All the stress from her head and shoulders melted, trickling into her chest, over her belly, and down her thighs.

She sighed as she pried open one eye. "You realize you're talking yourself right out of any chance at sex, don't you? I have to get back to work, sooner rather than later. The longer we talk, the less time we have."

He seemed to think about it, the corner of his mouth lifting, and then he nodded his head. "That's okay. There's more to you than your body." He kissed her forehead. "Besides there's always tomorrow, and now that I have a working refrigerator, the whipped cream will keep."

With both eyes open, Nel stared at the man who up-ended her world a little over a month ago. Before Grey, she figured a ridiculously successful, Will-Fortune-crushing business and a quiet, docile man at her side were the keys to her happiness.

But lately, she was pretty damn happy without those two things. With only Grey.

There's always tomorrow, he said. The words and his incredible patience with her miserable mood made her wonder things she shouldn't be wondering, like was he as blindsided by feelings beyond sex as she was? And then immediately none of it mattered, because his words weren't accurate. They would run out of tomorrows—soon. And that sucked worse than finding Tawny Kellogg on his front stoop.

Nel swore she wasn't going to let feelings get in her way, but she had it bad for him. So bad she opened her mouth and said, "I don't like that woman."

"I don't either," Grey said without hesitation.

"Good." It was a simple word, but it weighed heavy on Nel's tongue. And when he smiled, slow and sly, the implication made her heart cringe. He knew she was jealous, didn't he?

Panic surged into her throat, but then she stuffed it down with a so what? She liked him. He had to know she liked him. For crying out loud, they'd been sleeping together for three weeks. She didn't have sex with a man unless she liked him very much.

Seeing another woman fawning over Grey on his front porch simply meant Nel was territorial, not a needy, emotional mess. She could admit she didn't like Tawny because she liked Grey. Right? What harm would there be in such an admission?

Nel couldn't decide, so she took the safer approach. "I used to work for that agency."

The rest of it, including unavoidable details about her relationship with Will, spilled out over the next half hour. On one hand, rehashing her greatest heartbreak wasn't an enjoyable way to spend an afternoon, but on the other hand, the man sitting beside her in a lawn chair on the back patio, throwing a ball for two eager dogs, made it seem like the absolute best way to spend an afternoon.

"Now, see, I might not like her, but I like him," Grey said, grinning.

"Will? He's an asshole."

"Exactly, and I like that about him, because if he wasn't, you wouldn't be here with me." He heaved the ball into the brush at the back of the yard, and the dogs bolted. "Well, maybe you'd still be here as my realtor, but I wouldn't be able to do this."

He slid a hand beneath her hair and palmed her neck, pulling her closer until their lips met. Soft, slippery, and soul-shattering. When Nel opened her eyes, her head was spinning.

Grey simply smiled.

Something was happening here. Something had changed between them. But what? How? When? Maybe she was crazy. Maybe the endless work around this house while she tried to manage other business obligations had skewed her perspective.

The dogs barreled toward them again, Joker with the coveted prize. She watched bleary-eyed as Grey tugged the ball from the animal's mouth and launched it again.

"So selling this house and staking a claim on this neighborhood is your revenge on Will?" Grey leaned forward, resting elbows on his knees.

She stared at his strong, dark profile. Revenge wasn't the right word. She didn't feel very vengeful anymore. Mostly, she just wanted to be successful to prove she could be.

"It'll make a statement," she finally said.

Grey turned his head to look at her, and after a painfully long pause, he nodded. "I'm glad I can help you do that. I never got to make a single statement to Lindsay after she ran off with my dad." He turned to face the charging dogs. "Now it's too late."

Nel couldn't imagine how hard it was to not have closure. She still got a power trip from remembering Will's face the day she walked out of his office and his life. Every wronged lover was entitled to that.

"I'm sorry," she said, wishing she could say a few words to Lindsay, too—and Grey's father while she was at it.

"Don't be. At least I don't ever have to see her again."

Blackjack sat and dropped the ball at Grey's feet. Joker sat, too, closer to Nel. She reached out and smoothed the fur made softer by weeks of good food and care. "Yeah, running into Will is not fun, but I manage. It's bound to happen in the small world of Pittsburgh real estate."

"Do you see him a lot?" A muscle in Grey's cheek twitched.

Her heart flipped. It shouldn't have. Imagining Grey felt any amount of possession toward her was contrary to her ability to remain even-keeled and level-headed when it came time for him to leave. And he was going to leave. And she wasn't going to follow him. There was no way around it.

"No," she said, holding back a sigh. "Fortunately, Will stays in the North Hills most of the time and has his minions work down here. But I'll see him this weekend. We're both being recognized at Pittsburgh Real Estate's yearly awards gala."

The twitch in Grey's cheek calmed, and he returned to a slow, rhythmic bobbing of his head. "Congratulations on the recognition. What's it for?"

Nel cringed. "Pittsburgh Real Estate's Female Mover and Shaker."

It was such a stupid name. She didn't want to seem ungrateful, but more than the name, she hated the idea of Will garnering the evening's biggest award, walking in there as king of the real estate world, while everyone still viewed her as a start-up. By the end of the night, Will's smug smile would be emblazoned on her brain, and the only way to get rid of it was to knock him off the podium and replace his smile with a frown when she was named Broker of the Year instead of him.

That would take a lot of work and God only knew how many years…unless she could capitalize on this house. She glanced over her right shoulder at the stone structure, and then back to Grey. As much as she loved spending time with him, he'd be gone soon, and her hopes for a clean break were fading. He was occupying more and more of her head—and heart—leaving less time for thought about her business. Sure, listing this house was the catalyst for her master plan, but at what price? Now, more than ever, she was certain she needed to cultivate some personal distance to preserve her professional success.

But the longer she looked at the man in question, the clearer it was she couldn't follow through. Giving up any of the time they had left together seemed cruel.

Nel smiled and smoothed her hand down the soft flannel covering his back. "Thank you."

He smiled at her from over his shoulder. "For what?"

"For making me talk," she said, her fingers curling until her nails dragged along his back. "I feel better." She was sabotaging herself, knowing the gesture was meant as more than reinforcement of her gratitude.

What was it about this man that made her lose her mind?

She stood then, battling with herself over the same tired reasons. He was going. She was staying. Whatever this was couldn't last. "I should get back to the office," she said. "Lunch is over."

Grey sat back and reached for her hand. "I was hoping you could forget about work."

Funny, she was hoping she could forget about him. But since that wasn't going to happen, today seemed as good as any to take the rest of the day off.

CHAPTER THIRTEEN

"I can't believe you won't come see your nephew."

Tired of the same old conversation, Grey leaned on the granite countertop. "It's not that I won't. I can't." He still had two bathrooms to remodel and a truckload of Dad's junk to move out.

"Are you in prison?"

Looking around the completed kitchen and into the gleaming great room, Grey thought about the hell he'd walked into six weeks ago. Back then, it felt like a prison. Not so much now.

"You caught me," he teased. "But they're allowing me to have my cell phone on account of good behavior."

"Be serious."

"You're the one who brought up prison."

A heavy sigh came from Jordon's end of the phone. "Grey, where are you? And before you say Nashville, think again. Hoffman had meetings at the stadium last week and he stopped by your place, hoping to take you for a beer, said he found a Fed Ex slip stuck to the door dated a month ago."

Grey took a deep breath and delayed his exhale, holding in a groan. He couldn't keep the truth from Jordon much longer, and he shouldn't have to. The house was days from being done. Hell, if he spent less time in bed with Nel, he'd be done already, the house would be listed, and he'd be holding his baby nephew in one hand while he beanbag tossed on Jordon's lawn with the other.

That had been the plan before he learned the terms of Dad's will. Plans changed, and now there was this house…and Nel. A part of Grey was dragging his feet when it came to finishing up and leaving, but he couldn't defer forever.

He was expected in Tampa in two weeks.

It was time to face facts. With Nel's brothers' help, this house could be done in a few days, four max. Then Grey could head south, stopping off at Jordon's on the way.

"I'll see you next week," he said, ignoring the cloud of uncertainty hanging over his head.

"Fine, but when you get here I'm going to ask you again where you've been, and it's going to be a lot harder to brush me off in person."

True. Grey knew hoping for the house to sell before he arrived at Jordon's was too much to ask, but a part of him did anyway. It would sure make things easier. Knowing a supersonic sale wasn't going to happen, he'd just have to keep up his dubious ways. It would all be worth it once he handed Jordon the check, like their father should've done all those years ago. Then they'd be that much closer to closing the door on the old man's memory and driving in the bolt lock. Then, only making things right with Tag would be left.

An hour later, as Grey laid tile in the master bath, he contemplated everything from shipping the dogs back home to Nashville and finding them in-home care, to leaving Nel and when he would see her again. She said he didn't need to be present for closing once the house sold. He probably couldn't be present even if he wanted to. The season would be in full swing, and he'd be God-only-knew where. But he'd be back here in Pittsburgh for a three-game series in May. He could see her then.

May seemed so far away.

The more he thought about it, the more he was convinced he needed to make what remained of their time together memorable enough to hold them over to May. After all, as much as he didn't like his father, the crash taught Grey about the fleeting nature of life. Here one day, gone tomorrow. Memories—good and bad—were what remained. It was a sappy notion that made him more than a little uncomfortable.

The high-pitched whirring of the tile saw cut off his thoughts, and for the next two hours he was too preoccupied with measuring, cutting, and grouting to think of much else. But when he walked into the master bedroom where his father's clothes piled high upon the king-sized bed, he was hit with genius.

A tuxedo. What if he donned the fancy duds and showed up at Nel's awards ceremony unannounced? He could stand in the back of the room, watch her receive her award and then treat her to an overnight stay at the priciest hotel in town. There'd be champagne, roses, chocolate-dipped strawberries—and whipped cream.

He grinned. See? He could do this romantic thing.

He could also be recognized. The grin faded, but then something sensible surged in his overprotective brain. At this point, who cared? The house was basically finished. And if word got out he had a woman in Pittsburgh, it didn't seem like such a big deal anymore. Maybe because it was Nel. She had a way of making him feel like sharing anything with her—including *TMZ*'s front page—was a win. Besides, she wasn't famous, so really, who but the locals would care? The locals didn't talk to Jordon. And even if they did, he wanted to believe Jordon would be happy he'd moved past Lindsay. Then again, if Jordon's tendency to overprotect a client made him question Nel's motives for being with Grey, it would still be a great distraction from the house. Grey could tell him he'd met someone—someone special—and that was why he'd been so secretive about where he was.

It sounded like a foolproof plan to Grey.

With a nod, he settled his thoughts on giving Nel a night to remember.

But first, he needed to try on the tux.

•••

"I hate these things." Nel inhaled and sucked in her gut so Rena could zip up the back of her ball gown.

"Then why are you going?"

"You know why I'm going. If I don't go, Will wins." Nel fastened a crystal necklace around her neck.

"Will already won Broker of the Year. There's nothing you can do about that."

She stared at Rena's reflection in the mirror. "That's not the win I'm talking about."

Rena spun her around by the bare shoulders. "Don't make this night about him. Find something else to focus on or you're going to be miserable. And if you're miserable, your father's going to kill him."

Nel laughed. "Dad will have to get in line behind the boys." Her brothers hated wearing suits and ties, but they wouldn't miss the opportunity to support her *and* death-stare Will for the world.

The idea of such shenanigans made attending the ceremony tolerable, but she'd rather be spending the evening with Grey. Once again, she reminded herself he'd soon be gone, but her business would remain. There really was only one focus here.

With more help from Rena, Nel's curls were swept to the top of her head and her eyelids were dusted with shadow. She finished just as Dad and Mom pulled up to escort her downtown.

An hour later, sitting at a table in the front corner of the Westin ballroom, surrounded by her family, Nel felt incredibly blessed.

Across the way, Will was circled by his agents—mostly female, Tawny included—and he smiled and laughed until she expected his head to pop off from all the exuberance. Will Fortune was not exuberant—not really. He faked those things. Underneath the happiness act was a man who was never satisfied.

Thank God she walked away when she did. If she hadn't, her life could've revolved around him.

Reaching into her silver handbag, she lifted her phone enough so she could see the screen. She had this silly idea Grey would text, but there hadn't been a peep, which was probably a good thing. Bit by bit, she'd let her guard down until she couldn't lie to herself anymore. He meant as much to her as anything, but unlike most things she held dear, she was going to have to let him go.

"How about another glass of wine," Mom said, leaning closer to Nel. "Your father's going to grab me one."

Nel smiled and patted her mother's chiffon-cloaked lap, and then looked at her father. "I think I'll pass. I have a speech to give, you know? It won't look very good if I'm slurring my way through it."

Mom covered Nel's hand with hers and squeezed as Dad walked away. "Even if you did slur, we'd think you looked good. You're our beautiful baby girl." She grinned. "And we're so proud of you."

Looking into her mother's sparkling eyes, Nel filled with satisfaction. Next to making herself proud, making her parents proud was the best feeling in the world. "I know you are," she said, leaning in for a hug.

"To the best real estate agency in town," Rick said, raising his pilsner glass.

The rest of her brothers followed.

Mom pushed Nel away. "Wait! I only have water, and we shouldn't toast without your father. It's not the same without him."

Or Grey. It was such a sudden, outlandish thought Nel grabbed her wine and drank more than she intended to.

"Come on, Mom," Rick coaxed. "We'll toast again when Dad gets back. To Nel and Parker Properties."

Glasses rose, then met with mouths around the table. Nel tried to think of something short and sweet and thankful to say for the impromptu toast, but her brain kept tripping over thoughts of Grey. How she wished he was here; how she wished she was there.

By the time Nel set down her glass, it was empty.

"She's going to need another glass." Joe grinned and then faced the crowd, craning his neck. "Dad's on his way back already, so I'll get it. Anybody else need anything?"

Warm tingles kissed the tip of Nel's nose as the rush of wine settled in her body. If she drank any more, she'd be on her ass. "Not necessary," she said to Joe and then held up her water goblet. "I can toast with this. Really." She took a drink on principle.

The ice water cooled the flush from the wine and Mom distracted her with a question about the red-headed realtor sitting to Will's left.

The evening continued uneventful until Paul said, "Hey, that looks like Grey Kemmons against the back wall."

To which Nel snapped her head away from the redhead at Will's table with enough force she pulled a muscle in her neck. *Ouch!* She pushed a palm into the burning spot and tried to see, through watering eyes, the man who would make Paul say such a thing.

"It *is* Grey Kemmons," Rick said before Nel got a good look, and then Rick stood, waving his arm overhead, blocking her view.

Nel leaned farther to her right, still cupping her neck, still trying to find this mystery guy her brothers thought was Grey. The pain in her neck no longer crippled her movement, but a strangling sense of anticipation robbed her of breath, and her head felt ten sizes too big.

Her father approached the table with a glass of wine and a tumbler of tonic water in hand, and then, over his right shoulder, Nel saw the most beautiful man, a vision dressed in a silver-gray tuxedo, a white shirt opened at his throat.

Paul was on his feet, walking toward Grey.

Nel hyperactively blinked and swallowed as she watched it unfold. Was this really happening? The vision dwarfed everyone else in the crowd as he made his way to the table, an almost bashful, crooked smile on his crisp clean-shaven face.

Sweet baby Jesus. Stunned. That's what she was. *Why was he here* entered her brain, but as her brothers got up from the table to fawn over him, and her mother's hand latched onto her wrist, Nel's brain failed.

"*Who is that?*" Mom asked.

"Grey Kemmons?" Dad questioned, scratching his bald head.

"Who's Grey Kemmons?" Mom released Nel and grabbed hold of Dad.

"Baseball," Nel whispered.

"How does Paul know Grey Kemmons?" Dad stood, tossing his napkin to his seat.

The boys herded Grey closer to the table. His smile grew weaker then, and he looked downright scared as he made eye contact with Nel. She meant to smile to reassure him, but she was frozen stiff.

"Evening," he said. "I apologize for crashing the party."

Nel's mouth hung open. Cool air from the room chilled the inside of her cheeks, and she tasted food she hadn't eaten on her limp tongue.

Mom's hand gripped her wrist again. "Good evening, young man," Mom said.

"Take my chair," Rick said. "I'll scrounge up another." Rick pulled out the chair beside Nel.

She closed her mouth and blinked as Grey made his way around the table to settle in Rick's seat. And by the time he sat, staring at her expectantly, she was long overdue to speak.

A smile lifted her lips. "You came," she whispered.

"I did." His voice was just as low and intimate. "I hope that's okay. I didn't realize it was a family affair." His eyes shifted away from her face, and his mouth twisted, but then he looked at her and ran his gaze from her head to her emerald silk-covered lap. "You look amazing," he breathed.

Joy rushed Nel's veins and for a split second, having forgotten where she was, she moved in for a kiss. But then Mom's grip tightened on her wrist.

They had an audience. *Crap*.

Nel directed a wider, forced smile at her parents. "Mom and Dad, this is Grey Kemmons. Grey, meet George and Ellen Parker."

Nel leaned back as Grey's strong arm reached across her to shake her mother and father's hands.

"It's a real pleasure. I've been watching you play since you were with Cincinnati," Dad said.

"How do you two know each other?" Mom asked.

And suddenly Dad's eyes were sharp, full of inquisition, and directed at Nel. "Good question, Ellen."

"We're helping him renovate a house," Paul said from across the table.

Paul probably figured he was helping the situation, but by the looks of Dad's now-suspicious eyes trained on Grey, the interjection upped the apprehension.

"So you're business associates?" Dad asked.

"Dad, please…"

"It started out that way," Grey interrupted, clearing his throat repeatedly.

His nervousness was endearing, while his directness was confusing. He'd never been the most forthcoming person.

Nel tossed him a raised-brow, inquisitive glance wrapped in a smile, when what she really wanted to do was ask point-blank, "What are you doing?"

With a shrug and a smile of his own, he rested a hand over Nel's, laced their fingers together and lifted their joined appendages onto the table.

A little noise escaped from Mom, and Dad's eyes widened. Nel didn't even breathe. She *had* to be dreaming.

A clanging rose from the front of the room. "If you will all take your seats, we'll get started with the awards presentations."

That was it. The lights in the room dimmed, and everyone angled their chairs toward the podium as the room quieted.

Nel could finally breathe, but the breaths were shallow and unsatisfying. Her hand, still clasped in Grey's, was resting in his lap. And although everything was incredibly confusing and surreal, everything felt one-hundred-percent right.

He came, and the things that that did to her. Stealing a glance at his clean profile washed in dimmed overhead lights, she swallowed a shot of desire and chased it down with some lingering confusion. He shaved. He appeared in public. He was risking recognition. For her? She couldn't think about what that meant, not now, not when she was about to stand in front of three hundred people.

Later. She'd get the answer to all her questions later.

With a breath, she settled into her seat, trying her damnedest to pretend nothing about the night was extraordinary. When it was time for Nel to accept her award and say a few words, she spoke directly to her family, thanking them for their support in her business venture. Seeing Grey among the people she loved most doubled the size of her heart, making the muscle ache for lack of space in her chest. More than once, she itched to rub the spot beneath her left breast, but she worried she'd be transparent, so she dealt with the ache and swallowed all the mushy words her heart wanted her to say. For the rest of the evening, she talked, smiled, and laughed, while fighting tooth and nail to suppress the truth.

She loved him.

"Excuse me, Mr. Kemmons. Can I get your autograph for my nephew?"

The stranger's voice struck dread in Nel, and she immediately looked at Grey's face to see how he responded to the recognition. He closed his eyes briefly, so briefly maybe no one noticed it as anything more than a blink, but she knew. She saw the barely perceptible pulse in his cheek, too, but when he opened his eyes and inhaled, the only thing she saw was his generous smile.

"Sure," Grey said, taking a pen and napkin from the man. "What's your nephew's name?"

"Mason." The man beamed from ear to ear. "He's a centerfielder, too. Little League."

Grey nodded as he scribbled something on the napkin and then handed it back. "Good luck to him. Tell him the trick is getting a good jump on the ball."

More people crowded the table. Grey's smile never faltered. He signed autographs for everyone, making baseball-related small talk. The memorabilia seekers looked every bit as smitten as Nel. She'd never seen this side of Grey Kemmons before, and it was intoxicating.

There was no way he'd be going home alone tonight.

"I'm going to ride with Grey," Nel said, leaning over Mom, making sure Dad could hear.

Her parents exchanged looks and then Mom patted Nel's thigh. "Have fun, sweetheart. Be careful, and remember how proud we are of you." She leaned in, placing a kiss on Nel's cheek.

Dad's untamed brows darkened his eye sockets. "You sure?"

Nel nodded. There were still so many things she was unsure of where Grey was concerned, but leaving with him tonight wasn't one of those things.

"Okay then." He reached across Mom and patted Nel's hand.

Twenty minutes later, Nel and Grey were alone in the thinning crowd, trying to make their way out of the ballroom. Hearty congratulations for Nel and curiosity over Grey stopped them every few steps.

And then the voice she would've been dreading—but expecting—all evening had she not been so wrapped up in Grey slithered into her ears, making the hairs on the back of her neck rise.

"Congratulations, Nel." Will stood with his arm around Tawny's non-existent waist. His fingers looked as though they were digging into his date's sequin-covered side, but they couldn't possibly be holding her as tight as Grey was holding Nel.

With Grey's arm locked beneath her breasts, crushing her back against his body, Nel couldn't take a full breath. "Thank you," she said, flashing a look at Will's smug face, but letting her gaze settle on the chandelier dripping from the ceiling behind him. "Congratulations to you as well." It was required to remain polite, and she did want things to be civil. Especially with Grey keeping watch, and especially now that Tawny was seeing Nel *with* Grey. The woman couldn't possibly be stupid enough to not recognize him—even without the beard.

Nel hoped for stupidity anyway.

"You clean up well," Tawny said smiling at Grey.

"I'm sorry. Have we met?"

Nel wanted so badly to wiggle her way around to see his face. Was he seriously trying to call Tawny's bluff? And was it actually working? Tawny's face scrunched, and she looked confused.

"*We* haven't met." Will thrust his free hand in Grey's direction. "Will Fortune, broker extraordinaire." He chuckled at his stupid joke.

"Greyson Kemmons, Gold Glove center fielder for the Nashville Argonauts." He didn't take Will up on the handshake.

Will's upper lip twitched, something that only happened when he knew he'd been beaten. Seeing it gave Nel way too much satisfaction, and she had to get away before she unleashed a bitchy smile.

She craned her neck and lifted her chin to Grey. "We should go," she whispered. And then she offered her most reserved smile to Will and Tawny. "Have a lovely evening. It was good seeing you."

Which was a total lie, but honestly, Nel didn't care. How could she worry about them when she had Grey?

CHAPTER FOURTEEN

"We're staying *here*? But I thought we were going home? I don't have clothes or my toothbrush or…"

Grey touched his finger to Nel's moving lips. "I had the concierge take care of the critical things."

"Oh." Her sparkling eyes pulled him in for a kiss, despite them being in full view of people leaving the ballroom.

After the run in with Good Old Will, Grey felt extra-possessive of Nel, and in an uncharacteristic display of his personal life, he didn't care who saw him kiss her outside the elevators.

On the other hand, what he wanted to do to her once they were *inside* the elevator required a bit of privacy.

"What about the dogs?" she asked when the kiss ended.

"Fed, watered, and let out before I left. They should be good until morning."

She nodded, blushing shock still on her face. "I can't believe you did all this." She reached up and touched fingertips to his cheek. "And you shaved."

He smiled as she trailed her nails over the ball of his cheek. "The beard looked a little shabby with the tux."

"Excuse me, but you're Grey Kemmons, aren't you?"

Grey dragged his gaze away from Nel's beautiful face to the wrinkled face of an old man. He should've been used to the recognition after the onslaught of admirers in the ballroom. And didn't he attract more attention by kissing her? But still…Being out in the open again caused a little patch of hives to spring up beneath his collar. He tucked a finger between the clothes and skin for a good scratch, and then managed a gracious smile. "I am."

"You're a good ball player. Got power like Puckett."

The elevator bell chimed, and Grey placed his hand on the small of Nel's back, urging her inside. "That's quite the compliment, sir. Thank you." Hopefully the guy had detoured from wherever he'd been heading to talk to Grey, and he wasn't planning to follow them.

The man stepped onto the elevator.

Grey bit back a sigh as Nel pressed into the corner, a goofy grin on her face. She'd been looking at him like that a lot tonight. He wondered what it meant while he punched the number six and asked, "What floor, sir?"

"Five."

It figured. So much for the high-intensity groping session Grey had planned. He didn't figure he could do much more than kiss Nel again in the space of one floor.

"How old are you?" the old man asked, staring hard at Grey's face.

"Twenty-nine."

"Used to be that was getting up there for a ball player, but these days guys are playing when they should be home watching on TV."

Grey nodded, laughing on the inside, thinking about how Nashville's forty-one-year-old shortstop would feel about that.

"Whatcha doing in Pittsburgh?"

Grey tensed. He knew fielding this question was only a matter of time, but now that the time had come, he wasn't terribly confident of his answer. He glanced at Nel, and there was a tight worry on her face. She pushed away from the wall, and any minute he expected her to come to his rescue. He loved that about her—she was fierce.

With his eyes locked on hers, Grey relaxed. "I'm here, spending time with my girl." Sure, they were words that took the heat off his real purpose for being in Pittsburgh, but right now, standing in this elevator, the words were also true.

The old guy nodded as the bell chimed for the fifth floor. "Have a nice evening, and good luck this season."

"Thank you," Grey called as the doors slid shut behind the man. And then Grey turned on Nel, hauling her to him with arms around her waist.

She gazed up with wide, bright eyes. "You're so nice to everybody."

"You look surprised." He played with a couple curls that escaped her sexy-as-hell hairdo.

"I am. I thought you hated being recognized, and you weren't that nice to me when we met."

Even though the elevator door slid open behind him, he cupped her face in his hands and brought her lips to his. "That's because I knew you were trouble." He backed her against the elevator wall and kissed the breath right out of her.

The door behind him slid shut, and still he kissed her. The elevator dropped into motion, surprising him with the downward direction, but still he kissed her. Only when the car jerked again did he come up for air—just in time for the doors to drag open and guests to step on.

Grey put an inch of space between him and Nel, his eyes glued to her reddened face. He had no idea how many people stood behind him or where they were going. It was hard to think rationally when the head in his pants was in charge.

Nel stretched past him on the wall side, probably to re-punch their floor number into the panel. He didn't much care. With her silky, full skirt crowding his body, he saw the perfect opportunity to prolong the pleasure.

When she settled back against the wall, he leaned closer, sliding a hand around her, using the miles of fabric from her gown to hide his destination and keep her decent. There was absolutely nothing wrong with a man putting his arm around his date while they stood face-to-face in a crowded elevator. Now, a man maneuvering his hand beneath the silky fabric covering his date's ass? That might be questionable. But with Nel wedged into the corner and blocked by the wall, her overflowing dress and his formidable body, who knew? By the look of her unreadable face, no one—except Grey. He knew, because his fingers were tracing the crack of her backside, and he saw her eyes glaze over, felt her breath hitch. And knowing made it hard for him to think straight. To keep it from going too far, too fast.

The elevator chimed its arrival, and there was movement behind him. He stilled with his hand cupping her ass, his fingers barely between her legs.

"They're gone," she whispered, her voice mixing with the sliding door.

He kissed her then, slipped a finger inside her warm, wet. She gasped into his mouth and arched against him.

The next stop was their floor, and they rushed through the hall in silence, hand in hand. A welcomed tension tightened Grey's body, and anticipation quickened his breathing. This woman managed to do something to him only baseball could ever do— when he was with her, he lost himself, lost the drama of his life, the disappointments, the tears, forgot every damn thing that didn't feel good, and she left him feeling better afterward.

Grey shoved into the room, pulling her behind him, but she stopped, giving resistance to his stride. "What?" he asked, turning to her, hoping he wouldn't see second thoughts playing out on her face.

She stared, wide-eyed, into the room. "This is amazing."

He looked where she was looking and admired the gentle glow of the fireplace flames flickering around the room. He wasn't one for fancy digs, so he wasn't one to debate the décor, but if Nel liked it, he liked it. Besides, once she was naked, he wasn't going to have eyes for anything else.

"I'm glad you like it," he said, tugging on her hand, pulling her deeper into the room. "I wanted to celebrate you."

"Us," she whispered, staring at him, something melancholy creeping across her face.

His heart twitched, and he knew she was thinking about him leaving. She had to be, because he was thinking about leaving, too. Wasn't that why he'd really done this? It wasn't about sex or some real estate award. It was about making damn sure she remembered him. When he was gone. When the Wills of her world came sniffing around and there wasn't a damn thing Grey could do about it.

"I don't want you to go." Her voice broke, and a tear slipped down her cheek.

He squashed the stream with his thumb and ground his teeth together, not knowing what to say. Before he could think of something, she lifted her chin and the corner of her mouth, and spread his tuxedo jacket open with her hands flattened against his abdomen.

"But you're not gone yet," she said, sliding her hands to the clasp on his pants.

And when she dropped to her knees amid waves of emerald satin, he was pretty fucking sure being here—now—trumped being anywhere else in the world.

Even centerfield.

•••

Nel watched him sleeping in the early morning moonlight. Seeing him like this was so different than seeing him post-sex in the afternoon. He looked softer somehow, more vulnerable, and she wanted to promise to fight any battle for him. She supposed that was what it meant to love someone.

With emotion clogging her throat, she slipped from beneath the sheets and padded naked to the bathroom. If she could keep him here she would, like some deranged fan. She'd lock him in this hotel room, chain him to that bed, and never, never let him go. But this wasn't some Steven King novel, and she wasn't a complete kook. So she'd let him go, and when the time came to watch him walk away, she wouldn't shed a single tear, because she went into this eyes wide open.

She showered and brushed her teeth with items provided by the concierge, and then she sat on the toilet, wrapped in a soft, thick towel, wishing for the strength to get through whatever came next.

A soft knock startled her. "Hey, babe, I hate to rush this, but we need to get rolling. I have to get back to the dogs."

Babe. It was the only thing Nel took away from the sentence.

Thirty minutes later, outfitted in last night's gown, Nel riding shotgun in Grey's pickup truck, they pulled into the driveway of her condo. "Thank you," she said, smiling brightly, despite the dread in her heart. She wasn't exactly sure what she was dreading more, the next goodbye or a full workday on a few hours' sleep.

"Thank *you*," he said, leaning across the seat and sliding a palm to her cheek. There was something sappy and oddly unwelcomed in the way he looked at her. All she could think was he loved her too, and they were both about to be destroyed by the wayward emotion.

Nel swatted his hand away. "Save it for lunch." She grinned as she pushed free from the truck. Light. Flippant. It was better this way. His departure date would be here soon.

She managed to keep that rational thinking while she dressed for work, but once she reached the office and came under the gun of Rena's questions, she weakened.

"You should tell him you love him," Rena said, tapping a pen against a memo pad.

"That'll only make it worse. You didn't see his face when I told him I didn't want him to go." Nel winced at the memory. "No way. I don't want him looking back at me with pity, like I'm some poor lovesick fool who fell under his spell."

"What if it's not a spell? What if he loves you, too?"

Nel dragged air into her mouth to put out the spark of excitement that lit beneath her breast. "It changes nothing. He's still going to Florida, and then to Nashville, and then wherever baseball takes him. I'm still staying here with my business and my family. I don't see how a relationship can work under those circumstances."

"That sucks."

"Tell me about it."

By lunch, Nel was hopped up on enough caffeine to stave off exhaustion, but the stimulant also put her mind in overdrive. Every other second she questioned the wisdom of spending her lunch hour with Grey. No matter how they spent the time, they'd only be deepening their doomed connection.

But like a freaking moth, she flew straight for the flame; only to find Tawny Kellogg's car in the driveway.

Nel almost drove past and returned to the office. She was too tired and wired to deal with it. Instead, she decided to end this stupid game. A little voice inside her head told her Grey could handle it, but this wasn't just about Grey anymore.

After last night, Will had to know Nel was involved with this house. Now Will needed to know she couldn't be chased off.

CHAPTER FIFTEEN

"I told you before, the house is not for sale." Grey stared down at Tawny, who forced her way into the foyer with a fake-ass trip.

"Listen, I'm sure you feel some obligation to Nel, but The Fortune Agency has a buyer. He's a hockey player, and he's willing to pay…"

"Leave."

"You don't mean that."

"I do." He didn't touch her, but he reached past her and forced the open door wider, banging the wall behind it.

She jumped.

She jumped again when she heard what came next.

"Will Fortune still doesn't do his own dirty work, does he?" A raging Nel threw open the screen door.

Cat fight came to mind, but it didn't hold an ounce of the appeal like it did when a guy tossed the word around the clubhouse. "She was just leaving," Grey said, hoping to smooth Nel's obviously ruffled feathers.

"Fine," Tawny huffed, flipping her hair. "Just know whatever's going on here is going to keep you from making a ridiculous amount of money on this house."

"What are you talking about?" Nel snapped.

Grey wished she hadn't taken Tawny's bait.

"We have a cash buyer."

Nel's eyes narrowed. "You're a liar."

"And you're a third-rate realtor who likes to play broker."

Grey jumped between the women, catching a lunging Nel in his arms, keeping the screen door from slapping her ass with the palm of his hand.

Tawny took her painted-on smile and waltzed out of his house.

Damn. Not exactly the afternoon he expected.

"I should've seen this coming." Nel scrambled from his arms and bolted into the great room with a throaty roar. "Of course he has a buyer. He's the official…" she formed air quotations with her fingers "…real estate agency for the professional teams in the area." She roared again. "Mother f—"

"Calm down," Grey said, crossing the room to her. "It doesn't matter, because I'm not selling to him."

She blinked double-time, shaking her head until the curls looked chaotic. "Why wouldn't you sell? He has a buyer—a cash buyer! Do you know what that means?"

Grey stared blankly.

"It means you could have money in hand faster than you can say *sold*, like by the time you leave. No sign in the yard. No open houses. Nada."

Wow. Under any other circumstances…

"Sounds good doesn't it?"

He reached for her, but she stepped back.

"You have to take it, Grey."

He stuffed a finger into his ear, because he certainly wasn't hearing her right. "What did you say?"

"Take the money and run." Her face crinkled when she said the words, but her eyes blazed with something that made him very uncomfortable.

What happened to the woman who fell asleep in his arms last night? The woman whose body all but begged him to stay before she drifted off amid contented sighs? The woman who made him lay awake, staring at the ceiling, wanting to stay beyond all reason.

Grey shook his head. "I won't. I can't do that to you."

"Why not? You're going to blow out of town and rarely think about me. Why let sex screw you out of the best possible deal?"

Strong words—words that pierced his heart—but then her eyes closed, and he saw them—her—for what they were, an attempt to do the right thing, the thing she thought was best for him. It was a sacrifice. She was willing to give up what she wanted so he could get what he wanted.

Had anyone ever done something so selfless for him? And she thought he could forget her …

He stepped to her again, and this time when she backed up, he caught her wrist and dragged her to him. "I'm going to think about you all the time." His right hand smoothed over the small of her back, pressing her to him. His left hand rode the curve of her shoulder to her neck.

"Liar," she whispered.

"I wish to God I was." Leaving her might kill him, because if it felt like this every damn time he thought of her, he wasn't going to survive the splitting pain in his chest.

She dropped her forehead to his chest and her shoulders heaved. "This is too hard."

He couldn't disagree, but he didn't release her. He held her tighter, until her muscles relaxed and she wrapped her arms around his waist.

"And I'm too tired to worry about it now. Maybe we could just nap for an hour." She looked up at him and yawned.

Sounded good to him, only he couldn't fall asleep. He stared at the ceiling for about twenty minutes and then pushed out of bed, leaving Nel to her dreams, hoping they were pleasant. If he managed to fall asleep, he was sure he'd have nightmares. He'd never been so conflicted. But regardless of his conflictions, there was still work left to do.

He made his way to the far side of the house where an unfinished bathroom tucked behind another bedroom. Hopefully he'd be far enough away so she couldn't hear him work.

Grey set the alarm on his phone in time to wake Nel, and then he settled into smoothing tile adhesive on the shower wall. He pressed marble subway tiles onto the adhesive in between yawns and wrist-rubs of his eyes. It really was surprising he couldn't fall asleep, considering how damn exhausted he felt.

On autopilot, he worked from the inside out, leaving space for pieces he needed to cut, filling the center in record time. Not wanting to stop if finishing was in sight, he moved to the tile saw, cutting precision pieces to fill the empty space on the wall. It was noisy, monotonous work, and in his current state, it wasn't easy. Rushing wasn't smart, but he wanted it done, so he pushed through the resistance, harder than he should've, and before the message to pull back traveled from his brain to his hands, he slipped, driving his hand into the blade until he heard it hit bone.

"Fuck!" It didn't sound like his voice, strangled in tears. He held his gushing right hand to his belly and raced from the room.

"Nel!" *Jesus*, his head spun. His stomach lurched, and the heat radiating from his throwing hand was enough to melt him. "Nel!"

Through fuzzy vision he saw her racing down the hall. "What? What…" She clasped a hand to her mouth. "Oh my God."

"Call Jordon." It was all he could manage before he dropped to his knees.

•••

Nel's instinct was to call nine-one-one before she called Jordon, but Grey insisted on the other way around. So after stumbling through an awkward minute-long conversation with Grey's brother, she dialed 911, even managing to stay coherent despite horror compromising her mental capacity.

While they waited for help, she held Grey, him strangling his towel-wrapped hand. Her *'it's going to be okays'* were met with gut-wrenching moans. By the time paramedics arrived, he was scarily still and silent.

Nel couldn't stop shaking. People rushed around him, blocking her view, but she didn't try to maneuver around them. She needed the reprieve from seeing him pale and scrunched with pain. That vision wasn't helping her stay calm, and she needed her wits about her to follow the ambulance to the ER.

That three-mile drive seemed to take hours. Pulling into visitor parking at the entrance of the emergency room, Nel thought about calling Rena to explain her absence from work, but her hands were shaking so badly she couldn't manage to tap the right contact on her phone.

She brushed tears from her eyes and scrambled from the car, dropping her phone, picking it up and nearly tripping over her feet. Somehow, she made it into the lobby and stood at the reception desk.

"May I help you?"

Words stuttered in her head, and a few unintelligible sounds escaped her lips before she managed a nod, and said, "Yes, I followed an ambulance here."

"Patient's name?"

"Greyson Kemmons."

"Have a seat in the waiting room and we'll let you know when you can go back."

Nel wandered to an empty seat in the corner, doing her best to swallow down the excess saliva filling her mouth. She needed to see him. What if things got worse in the ambulance? There'd been so much blood. Surely his life wasn't threatened, but she didn't know. She knew houses and real estate contracts—she didn't know veins and arteries. Tears burned the back of her eyes as she stared straight ahead.

Minutes passed; then hours. She was leaning against the wall when a short man in burgundy scrubs approached.

"You're with Mr. Kemmons?" he asked.

Nel jumped to stand erect. "Yes."

"Follow me."

They wound through the cool, barren, medicinal-smelling hallways until they reached a large room sectioned off with privacy curtains. Grey was behind the farthest curtain, sitting up in bed, clad in a hospital gown. Wires dripped from his arms and chest to monitors at his bedside. And his hand was wrapped.

He opened his eyes and held Nel's concerned gaze. His was a miserable, vacant look, and her heart shattered.

"Hey," she managed, walking to his side, smoothing a hand down his left arm, careful not to disrupt the IV protruding from the crook of his elbow.

He closed his eyes again and swallowed. She had the unwelcome feeling she had no business being here.

"I'm waiting for the hand surgeon," he said, sounding raw.

So many questions flooded her mind, but none felt appropriate to ask. She didn't want to upset him any more than he already was. They were both too old and too jaded not to understand the gravity of the situation. She didn't have to know baseball to know this injury would impact his ability to play.

"Are you in a lot of pain?" she asked.

He shook his head against the pillow. "They've got me pretty drugged up."

For some reason, it made her smile. With his eyes closed and his still relatively smooth face, he looked younger, almost child-like and heartbreakingly vulnerable. She leaned down and brushed a kiss across his clammy forehead.

"Jordon will be here soon."

She hoped it was the right thing to say. Having his brother and agent here to advocate for him should be a positive, but she expected Jordon to have questions—for Grey and for her. He seemed to hold back on the phone, only asking what was necessary.

"He's going to shit," Grey whispered.

"All that matters is you getting better."

"That's not all that's going to matter to him."

A man in a white coat pushed through a split in the curtain. "So, Mr. Kemmons, let's take a look at that hand."

Nel stepped back, giving the doctor space. Once again, her view was blocked, and she felt fortunate. As it was, the rustling of the bandages being removed tossed her stomach.

"Squeeze my fingers. Can you feel this here? How about here? Here?" The doctor's rapid-fire commands unsettled her more.

Only when Grey answered with a *no* did Nel crane her neck to see around the doctor. Grey's head was against the pillow and his face was lifted to the ceiling. She wondered if he was praying, and then she decided to say a few of her own.

"You've got a significant injury here, and we need more imaging to see the full extent. I'll be honest—I'm worried about a major bone issue. I'm wondering if the blood vessels are still functioning. Do we worry about blood supply loss to the thumb? But nerve injury is my biggest concern, so we're going to get an MRI to see exactly what we're dealing with. We'll probably take you to the OR first thing in the morning." The doctor patted Grey's leg. "Tell somebody if you're still in pain."

Grey simply nodded, and the doctor was gone, leaving Nel bewildered as to how she should help this broken man. She stepped to the bedside, and gripped his good hand. "What do you need me to do?"

He opened his eyes and a heavy sigh sagged his usually straight and strong shoulders. "I don't think there's anything anyone can do."

If there was one thing Nel hated it was feeling helpless. Someway, somehow, she was going to make things better.

• • •

It doesn't look good. Every time Grey closed his eyes and tried to sleep, he heard the hand surgeon's words. So despite being emotionally and physically exhausted, he stayed awake, staring at the building outside his window, listening to the monitors beeping, wishing Nel was here. But after six hours, someone had to check on the dogs.

She'll be back, he told himself, and then settled his head on the pillow for another attempt at sleep. He didn't know why he bothered. Even if thoughts about his career being over didn't keep him awake, the nurses checking on him every five minutes would.

"What the hell happened?"

Jordon. Grey opened an eye, hoping the chastisement would sting less if he wasn't completely engaged. "I had an accident."

"Accident, my ass." Jordon crossed the room, filling the all-white space with his wide body dressed in a black suit and overcoat. "I knew you were headed for trouble when you wouldn't tell me where you were."

Grey opened both eyes and frowned. "You think you could cut me some slack, considering I'm completely screwed here." He tried to lift his hand. Even though it wasn't painful, it felt too heavy to move.

Jordon sighed and dragged a chair to the bedside. "Dinardi has already talked to the hand surgeon here, so everyone will be on the same page when you get back to Nashville."

Nashville seemed so far away.

"We'll know more tomorrow," Grey said, sort of babbling to fill the nervous space.

"Yep." Jordon kicked his ankle over the opposite knee and looked at something on his phone. "Until then, we have plenty of time to talk about why the hell you're in Pittsburgh and who the hell Nel is."

Jordon's bristling directness wasn't unexpected as much as it was unappreciated, considering Grey's current state and inability to prepare answers. But really, facing the potential end of his career, what the fuck did any of it matter?

"I inherited a house from Dad, and I was getting it ready to sell."

Jordon's tanned face darkened in his usual response to anything having to do with Dad. "You were getting it ready? Why wasn't a qualified construction crew getting it ready?"

Grey closed his eyes and shrugged. "I like doing renos." It sounded like a question.

"I'm not buying it."

"Nobody is. It's not finished."

"Smartass, I'm not buying your story. Forgive me if I think there's more to it after you've been evading my questions about your whereabouts for almost two months now."

"Fine." Grey concentrated on the fleck of pain, the tiny burn left in his mostly numb hand. Maybe that would distract him from the pain of falling short on his plan for the house and paying back Jordon.

"Did you know he bought that house with your money?"

Silence. If it weren't for the throbbing in Jordon's cheeks Grey might have thought he didn't hear him. "I figured it was only fair to fix the place up, sell it, and give you back your money."

"Damn it, Grey." But Jordon sniffed, and then he looked away, and the uncharacteristic emotional behavior made Grey's chest cramp. "I wish you hadn't done that."

Grey followed Jordon's gaze to his injured hand.

"It seemed like the right thing to do." It *was* the right thing to do…this injury didn't change that.

"And Nel? How does she figure into this?"

Grey shook his head, wanting to pick his words carefully, knowing Jordon would be a lot harder on a woman he assumed was looking to benefit from one of his athletes—especially his brother, especially after Lindsay.

"She's important to me."

"How so? Where'd you meet her? How long have you known her? If she's so damn important, where is she now?" With each question, Jordon's voice deepened and grew louder until Grey was pretty sure a nurse would be checking on them any minute.

"You're here about my hand and my career, not my personal life. She'll be back, and you'll be civilized, or I'll tell Maggie you're being insensitive to me and my injury."

At the mention of his wife, Jordon rolled his eyes and huffed, but his shoulders relaxed, and Grey knew he'd won. This round.

There'd be more...rounds with Jordon, rounds with doctors, rounds with Nel. But if there was the slightest chance Grey could get back to where he was, he needed to be ready for a fight.

CHAPTER SIXTEEN

Nel stared at the unfamiliar ceiling, listening to the dogs snore. If she turned her head so her cheek rested on the pillow, and she breathed deep enough, she could smell the warm, clean scent of Grey.

But he wasn't here. For three nights he'd been a prisoner to medical machinery and nurse monitors, while Nel slept in his bed with the dogs so he had one less thing to worry about.

She still couldn't believe the hand surgeon's abysmal prognosis, even though she saw what he was talking about with her own eyes. Grey couldn't feel whole parts of his right hand. His throwing hand. And by the look on his brother's face, this wasn't the kind of injury most men came back from.

But Grey wasn't like most men.

A tear collected in the corner of her eye, and she reached up to rub it away. After seeing his pain, what did she have to cry about? She wasn't faced with losing the career she'd worked so hard to build. She wasn't souped up on morphine because she nearly cut off her hand.

Joker stirred, pawing the comforter until his head snuggled in the crook of her arm. She welcomed the comfort, and ached a little because Grey probably missed it, especially knowing they'd decided it was best for the dogs to remain with her indefinitely in Pittsburgh until he had full use of both hands.

He'd be discharged today, and then he'd be leaving, heading for Nashville, where team doctors could see the injury for themselves and plot a course for rehabilitation. It had all been laid out dryly and presented as non-negotiable by Jordon.

Knowing how much Grey loved those dogs, her keeping them meant she'd talk to him regularly and see him again at some point; but she didn't know when, and she didn't know how any of it would affect the relationship they managed to build these past two months.

She loved him. She was more certain now than ever before. And falling asleep in his arms the night of the awards ceremony, she was certain he loved her, too. But no matter how sure and strong, love couldn't fix everything.

Grey's career wasn't the only thing on the line, was it?

That foreboding feeling stayed with Nel as she dragged herself out of bed, went through the dogs' morning routine, and then headed home to shower and change. The feeling intensified when she walked into the hospital and came face-to-face with Grey's brother, a man who looked like he'd rather be staring down a firing squad than her.

"Good morning," she said.

Jordon bobbed his head and then hid his mouth behind a ludicrously small, disposable cup of coffee.

Nel tossed a dismissive smile and walked past him.

"He's with the nurse. She's going over the discharge notes."

The words and their implied meaning—she wasn't privy to that much information about Grey—stopped Nel cold. "Don't you think someone should be in there with him?"

"Not particularly. We'll be in Nashville in a matter of hours, and he'll have a whole new set of protocol."

He wasn't very nice, but she had experience dealing with prickly Kemmons men. "You don't like me, do you?"

He shrugged and raised the cup to his lips again. "I'm indifferent to you."

Cripes. She'd hate to see what he was like when he didn't like someone.

"The way I see it, you've served your purpose—whatever that purpose was—and you'll be little more than an ink smudge on the timeline of Grey's life once that house is sold. So, yeah, I'm indifferent."

Ouch. He made indifferent sound worse than being not liked.

"I'll see to it that you're reasonably compensated for the care of the dogs."

"I don't want your money."

"Oh, it's not my money, it's Grey's."

"I don't want his money, either."

Jordon stepped toward her. "Then what do you want?" He was big and strong and totally trying to intimidate her. He was also a carbon copy of Grey.

She softened...a bit. "I want your brother to play baseball again. Next to you, it means more to him than anything in this world."

Nel would've given up just about everything to know where she ranked on that list.

•••

Grey held the discharge papers in his only functioning hand. He couldn't remember a damn thing the nurse said. Frankly, he didn't care. The only thing anyone said that mattered was the hand surgeon saying *it didn't look good.* Jordon seemed to think they'd hear something different in Nashville. Grey couldn't muster enough hope to care about that, either. Not right now. Not with Nel walking into the room, pity painted all over her pretty face.

He hated this. Hated the way he was leaving her. Hated that he was too distraught over the possibility of never playing ball again to figure out what came next—for them. And why was he even in this position? Because he screwed up. He left that bed when he should've been lying there, holding her while she slept. Instead, he snuck off, tired and preoccupied, insisting on pushing through the rest of the renovations. Stupid. And now he was paying the price.

"Hey," she said, clasping her hands at her waist. "Jordon said to tell you he's pulling the car around."

"Hey." The urge to touch her got as far as his right elbow and died on the thought of raising his injured hand. How pathetic would that be?

"Sorry I'm late. Joker took forever to do his business." She wrinkled her nose, and he found himself thinking how much he was going to miss that.

"If you throw him a ball a few times, he'll go. Gets things moving."

She smiled. "I'll try that."

She'd have to because even if he stayed, he couldn't do it. Funny, the biggest ache was in his heart, not in his hand.

"I'll let you know what the doctors say."

"I'd appreciate it. And I'll keep you posted on the progress with the house."

It was all so cordial, so businesslike, so unlike the way they'd been right before the accident. A flash of anger tightened his jaw. After everything, on the cusp of goodbye, and all they could talk about was his hand and the house? He hadn't even thought about the house much, not since Jordon absolutely, positively refused to take any money from its sale.

Seeing it finished and sold didn't have the same allure, so he told her, "No rush now."

She nodded. "Okay. You just get better, you hear?" And then her straight-backed business-like demeanor crumbled. Her shoulders drooped and her head tilted as she closed the gap between them to lay a hand on his cheek. "I won't be happy until I see you larger than life on my big screen standing in the middle of centerfield."

Hollow. That's how he felt. Her hope felt somehow misplaced. He didn't know if he'd ever be happy again. Losing baseball, losing her; it didn't seem fair. God, he couldn't believe he was back in this place again. The same dark hole he'd fallen into after Lindsay left with Dad. But this time, Grey refused to stay there long. He didn't know how, but he'd find a way out.

Again he thought about touching Nel, but the execution seemed too awkward to bear, so he leaned in and pressed a kiss to her lips. As far as kisses went, it was chaste, but for the first time in days he felt something other than pain and despair. Something good was buried beneath layers of fear and exhaustion. Buried, but it was there. And it gave him hope.

When the kiss ended, Nel blinked up at him, strumming her thumb across his cheekbone, keeping the "something good" humming. "I know it won't fix anything. In fact, it might make things worse in the long run, but at the risk of not being able to say this to you in person for a long time…I love you."

The unexpected words sort of hung there between them, like a sky-high pop-up. When a ball was high enough on the horizon, lost in the sun, Grey sometimes panicked, and his eyes got this weird tremor, like he'd never get a lock on the ball. He felt like that right now, facing Nel's love, only instead of in his eyes, the tremor was in his heart. What was he supposed to do with an admission like that?

He hugged her, because it was at least something he could do to show her he appreciated her going out on a limb when he couldn't find the courage to do the same. He felt a lot for her. Maybe it *was* love. But he was feeling a lot of other things, too…dark things; troublesome things. Things that had nothing to do with her, and he couldn't wrap his head around any of it right now.

"It's okay," she whispered, a fierce sound, one that didn't hint at any vulnerability. "You've got a lot facing you."

How he wished he'd be facing it with her.

With his left arm wrapped around her shoulder, he led her from the room, down the hall to the elevators. She stepped out of his reach to push the lobby button on the control panel, but didn't return to his side. She smiled at him while they rode to the lobby in silence, and he couldn't help but think about the last time they were in an elevator together. An endless sadness swirled in his stomach.

When the bell rang and the doors slid open, Jordon was waiting by the revolving entrance. Grey didn't want Jordon's input on this goodbye, so he stopped and pinched the discharge papers between his right arm and right side, making an awkward grab at Nel with his left hand. It was a weaker grip than he was used to, but he still managed to haul her to him.

"I'll see ya," he said, kissing the top of her head. God only knew when. And Grey had no idea what sort of man he'd be then.

With her arms wrapped around his waist and his chin resting on the top of her, he closed his eyes and tried to soak her in, knowing when he walked out those doors with Jordon, nothing would feel good for a very long time.

• • •

Nel tossed a ball for the dogs that bolted from her side. She didn't throw it nearly as far or as hard as Grey did, but Joker and Blackjack didn't seem to mind. They wrestled mid-yard, battling for the prize, while Nel thought about Grey; about how strange it felt being here without him. Had it really only been a few days since the awkward-but-fierce goodbye at the hospital?

Sometimes—like now—she smelled him on the wind and had to fight the urge to spin around like an idiot. Other times, she swore she heard his heavy footsteps across the hardwood floors. Missing him was driving her crazy, but she had to believe it would get easier once she acclimated the dogs to her condo and moved on from this house.

"Your cell's ringing." Paul poked his head and arm around the French doors, wiggling the phone in his hands.

Nel attempted a whistle, which failed miserably. "Blackjack, Joker, come." The artificially deep command was laughable, but it did the trick, and the dogs barreled toward her. She ushered them into the house while she grabbed the vibrating phone with the other.

She didn't recognize the out-of-area caller, but her fluttering heart had her hoping it was Grey. When she answered, he confirmed it with a *hey, babe*.

Every single time she heard his voice, she melted. It didn't matter where he was, where she was, or what was facing them, as long as he called her *babe*, she had hope they could somehow, some way, be happy together.

"Hey," she said, smiling into the phone. "How's Nashville?"

"Rainy."

"There's a five-degree wind chill here, and still I was outside throwing a ball." She chuckled, but the sound caught in her throat when he was silent. It was a stupid, insensitive thing to say. Surely he'd weather anything to be throwing a ball.

"I'm glad they're doing well for you," he said.

"They are. I love 'em to pieces." She smiled weakly, because she loved him, too, but not hearing him say it back was more than a little deflating.

Nel tried not to let Grey's lack of openness about his feelings bother her. She reminded herself over and over again what happened between them was never supposed to be long-term. Her loving him was an accident that didn't change the temporary nature of their time together—even if he loved her in return. What good would come of knowing he loved her, too, if they couldn't be together? Still, she hoped, somehow ...

"I'm going to North Carolina for a while," he said.

"Oh." Sadness displaced the joy she'd felt when she'd first answered the phone and heard his voice. For a minute there, somewhere between *I'm going to* and *North Carolina* she expected him to say *I'm going to come home*. Which made no sense whatsoever, because while he might be the owner of this house, it wasn't his home. And it most certainly wasn't hers.

"I have ten days before I start rehab here, and I need to see my new nephew. Plus, Jordon needs to get home and he's refusing to leave me alone."

"I think that's a great idea." For the first time since Nel met Jordon, she heartily agreed with him. The idea of Grey facing any of this alone thickened her sadness.

Her brothers buzzed around behind her, digging through the cupboards for the snacks she kept on hand while they finished up around the house. Joe nudged her aside to get to the fridge.

"Is that Grey?" he asked.

Nel nodded.

"Tell him if he wants us to keep working for him, he's going to have to shell out for a keg-o-rator. It's getting tiresome lugging in cases of beer."

Grey actually laughed. "Tell him I heard that, and if his drunk ass gets hurt on the job, there's no disability."

Nel cringed. She didn't want to think about anyone else getting hurt on this job. "You can tell him yourself," she said, passing the phone to Joe.

While the men chatted about the progress on the house, Nel paced the kitchen, roughing hands over her face. Thank God she had an open house to prepare for tomorrow. That should keep her mind somewhat productive, not that being here, cleaning out the house, taking care of the dogs wasn't productive.

But work kept her moving forward. Being here seemed to hold her back.

Joe thrust the phone in her direction, and she drew a deep breath before speaking. "Okay. Have a safe trip and a wonderful time with your nephew."

"I'll call you."

"Okay." Too many *okays* when everything was anything but.

• • •

The Nashville Argonauts announced today that Grey Kemmons will not be reporting to spring training due to a non-baseball related injury. Argos' staff refused to specify the injury or surrounding circumstances. Kemmons is expected to miss…

The television screen went black.

"Hey, I was watching that," Grey said to whomever was standing behind him while he lounged on the couch.

"Why would you want to?" Maggie rounded the sofa, the baby strapped to her chest with help from a psychedelic-print stretchy fabric.

Shit. She was going to lecture him, but he could handle the lecture just as long as she didn't get out the Play-Doh and start looking for hidden meanings in his sculptures.

He closed his eyes and shook his head. Having a psychotherapist for a sister-in-law was…interesting. "You're right. I don't want to watch it." Conceding was his best bet at peace.

Still, Maggie sat, and Grey caught a glimpse of his nephew. He was more comfortable around dogs, but he had to admit, holding Braydon was pretty cool. The kid's pale pink face wrinkled, and he squealed like a tiny pig. The sound made Grey smile. But then Maggie lifted her shirt and offered the kid her breast, and that made Grey look the other way.

"Have you thought about what happens after baseball?" she asked.

After baseball? As if there were such a thing. Baseball was like God—it always was, and always would be. But the more Grey sat with her words, the more he understood what she was asking, and it wasn't like he hadn't had these conversations with Jordon before. "My investments are strong. Jordon and I have talked about broadcasting, restaurants, a bunch of business opportunities. Basically, I'll pick one."

"Huh." She sort of stared off into space while the baby made smacking sounds that made Grey's skin crawl. "It doesn't sound like any of it elicits much excitement in you."

He shrugged. "If I need excitement, I'll sky dive."

Or spend the afternoon in bed with Nel. *That* would be his preference.

Dreams of Nel were keeping him up at night, making him miss her more each day. He thought limiting his contact with her would help keep her off his mind so he could think about what came next as far as his career was concerned. But thinking about what came next didn't change anything that was happening now. He still couldn't feel what he was supposed to feel. He could barely keep a baseball in his resting hand. Rehab might help, but he was days away from it, and weeks of grueling work would have to pass before he could know if any of it made a damn bit of difference.

"Tell me about Nel."

Grey side-eyed Maggie. Jordon couldn't keep his mouth shut when it came to his wife. She had him under one hell of a spell, which Grey was normally thankful for, considering without her Jordon may have never picked up the phone and prompted this reconciliation.

"I don't want to talk about it," he said.

She nodded. "Usually when we don't want to talk about something it's a pretty good indicator we should."

Bah! He threw up his proverbial hands. He should've known Jordon dragging him to North Carolina was an excuse for one big shrink session. "Fine. She's a realtor who found my dogs, returned them to my house, and helped me fix up the place."

Maggie nodded again. "She's staying at your house with the dogs, right? Something about the way she lingered on the word *your* made him sit up and pay closer attention to her words—and his.

"Yep. They took a liking to her after she found them and with all the time she spent with them."

"And how about you? Did you take a liking to her what with all the time you spent together?"

"Jesus, Maggie, this is stupid."

She laughed. "You are so much like your brother."

That made him smile. After everything in his past and through everything in his present, at least he had Jordon. It felt good to have family to count on. But then suddenly, that thought and Maggie's proximity and companionship made him miss Nel more fiercely than before.

Grey closed his eyes and took a swipe at his clammy forehead. "She loves me," he admitted for no damn good reason.

"Do you love her?"

It was the one question he'd been avoiding. "Maybe—I don't know. It feels so different than when I was with Lindsay."

"How so?"

He should've hated Maggie's intrusive questions, but it felt so good to talk about Nel—the next best thing to seeing her. He released a long, slow breath out his mouth, letting his shoulders fall and his head sink deeper into the pillow. "With Nel, it's easy. We just sort of go together. She calls me on my shit. I call her on hers. We work side-by-side for hours with nobody blowing up." His eyes were closed, and he was seeing her, remembering everything, and his lips stretched into the biggest smile. "See? She makes me smile…even when I have no reason to."

"That's great." At the sound of Maggie's voice, Grey opened his eyes and watched her lift Braydon onto her shoulder. "She sounds lovely."

She sounded perfect to Grey. And in that moment, he knew exactly how to answer Maggie's original question: *Have you thought about what happens after baseball?* He'd had a great baseball career—and who knew? Maybe he would again—but he'd never had a great family life.

Nel was his best shot.

CHAPTER SEVENTEEN

Nel dragged the garbage cans to the curb in front of Grey's house, lamenting the fact she was still hanging around, splitting her time between her condo and here. *Why?* She tightened her grip on the handle, focusing on the burn, not wanting to answer the question.

The god-awful sound of the plastic scraping cement made her cringe as she walked into a gust of chilly wind. When the world around her quieted, she noticed she wasn't alone. A wrinkled woman, dressed in nothing but a housecoat and walking with a cane, pulled a recycling bin to the curb of the house next door.

"Let me help with that," Nel called, starting off toward the woman with a little jump.

"Oh, I think I can manage." A sweet smile further wrinkled her face. "It's the only exercise I get these days. By the looks of me, you wouldn't know I used to run marathons, but I'm not doing half-bad for ninety."

"Ninety!" Nel reached the woman's side and grabbed the opposite corner of the bin. "That's amazing. You look great."

"Thank you."

They deposited the bin on the curb, and the woman turned to Nel. "You're working hard on that house."

"Yes." Nel shot a look over her shoulder at Grey's transformed home. "I am."

"It's good to see young blood move into the neighborhood. The circle of life, you know?"

The assumption pinched at Nel's heart. "It's not my house. I'm…" What came next grew harder every day. What was she to Grey? His lack of recent communication chipped away at her hope for the impossible. "I'm the realtor," she said, lifting her chin to exaggerate the pride in her profession rather than the ache in her heart. "The house should be on the market very soon."

The older woman's penciled-on eyebrows furrowed. "You do a lot more than the average realtor."

Nel chuckled. "Because I'm not the average realtor." If the woman only knew how much more she'd done for this house and this owner ...

"You ever hear the saying the Lord works in mysterious ways?" The woman momentarily raised her eyes to heaven.

"My grandmother used to say it."

"Smart woman." Again with the wrinkle-producing smile. "I said it because I just got off the phone with my sister in Florida, and I've decided to move in with her. Who knows how much time I have left, and why shouldn't it be spent somewhere warm? The only thing holding me back is this house. You interested in helping me sell it?"

Was Nel Parker interested in listing *any* property, let alone one like this? She looked at the pristine Colonial, spanning a double lot. "I'd kill to list it." She laughed, just to make sure she didn't scare the woman off with the macabre humor.

"How about you come by tomorrow morning around eight for coffee and a tour?"

"It's a date," Nel said, smiling.

She stayed smiling all the way to work. It was a nice change from sadness as her default emotion. Surely this was a sign her heart would go on after Grey was completely gone from her life. She didn't need him to be happy. But that didn't change the fact she wanted him.

Well, people didn't always get what they wanted, did they? She couldn't help think about how badly she'd wanted to be partner at The Fortune Agency, and look how that worked out.

Around noon, her smile was a distant memory, especially when financing fell through on a property set to close in one week.

"I'll see what I can do, Mrs. Ring. Another lender may have the same aversion to self-employment income, but I'm not giving up on this closing. I have a few connections at a couple local banks. Let's give them a try."

When the call ended, Nel turned her attention to Rena, who'd been waiting patiently, an anxious look on her face. "What? Dear God, you look like you're going to burst."

Rena exploded from her chair with a shriek. "Will was arrested."

"What?" Nel yelled, with an intensity that burned her face.

"Mortgage and wire fraud or something like that. It's all over the news." She skipped back to her desk and hunched over her laptop. "Come. Come."

Nel couldn't feel her feet touching the ground as she made her way to Rena's desk. All she could think or say was, "Oh. My. God."

Rena read an article aloud, and when she'd finished, Nel was speechless. Will had been submitting fraudulent mortgage applications to lenders for years, which meant Will was engaging in illegal business practices right under her nose.

His partner John Evans had been arrested, too. *That* could've been Nel. Not that she would've knowingly done something illegal, but what if Will brought her on as partner and kept the fraud from her? She'd be ruined by association, just like all the agents who were about to lose their jobs when the agency closed.

"Do you know what this means?" Rena asked, gripping Nel's limp hand. "You won! The battle of Will-versus-Nel is over. He can't compete from behind bars." Her laugh was maniacal.

Nel couldn't enjoy the personal satisfaction, because the business woman kicked into gear. "I was thinking it meant hundreds of acres of prime Pittsburgh real estate is about to be without a listing agent."

"That too!" Rena squealed. "You better get to work, girl."

Nel shuffled back to her desk, the chaos of the moment playing out in her head. Will was arrested. The Fortune Agency was closing. *Holy shit.* What to do first? Who to call? Could she waltz up the front walk of former Fortune Agency listings and offer to be their new agent? Was that like ambulance-chasing?

"You know what else this means?" Rena's voice filtered through the mental noise. "Next year, Broker of the Year belongs to you."

It could happen. It was in reach. After all these years, she saw an opening. Winning sounded so good. Winning would feel good, too; owning the title, walking up to the podium, giving an acceptance speech without Will in the room.

If only it wouldn't feel so bad not having Grey there either.

• • •

"You told me rehab is rehab wherever I do it as long as the therapists are qualified." Grey stared at the smoky lake behind Jordon's house and snuggled deeper into his hooded sweatshirt. Just because he knew he wanted to be with Nel didn't make the logistics of being with her fall neatly into place. He still had a less-than-functioning right hand and a baseball career to think about.

"I told you that before I knew you were asking because you were thinking about going back to Pittsburgh." Jordon adjusted the stocking cap on a sleeping Braydon's head. "I thought you were asking because you wanted to stay here with us for a while, but now that I know you're talking about going to Pittsburgh, I'm telling you Nashville is the best place for you to rehab. You'll have access to good therapists there."

"Let's be honest here. Is it that you *can't* arrange rehab in Pittsburgh because there aren't any good therapists, or you *won't* arrange it because you think Nel is a gold digger?"

Jordon looked up from the baby in his arms and stared across the patio table at Grey. "I don't know her well enough to know if she's a gold digger. Do you?"

Did he? Was two months of knowing someone long enough to know everything about them?

Grey thought about what he did know about Nel. He thought about her fiercely independent streak and the way she held him off until he thought he might explode from wanting her. He thought about how she went after what she wanted and how she gave herself completely when she finally let him in. He thought about her gut-wrenching honesty when she told him to take Will Fortune's deal—even though it would crush her—and again when she told him she loved him…even though he was in no shape to say it back.

And then he thought about her family and the way they rallied around each other like nothing he'd ever seen before, but something he was desperate to be a part of. As far as he was concerned, women didn't get better than Nel Parker. Maybe he didn't know everything about her, but he knew enough.

If he could just find the words to make Jordon understand, getting to Pittsburgh would be a lot easier.

Grey shook his head, and thoughts fell into place. "I knew Lindsay for ten years and thought I knew her as well as anyone could know a person, but apparently not. I had no clue she was a cheater."

"Exactly," Jordon said, nodding and then returning his attention to his son.

Okay, so that was the wrong approach.

Grey took a deep breath and regrouped, refusing to be frustrated. He didn't need Jordon's blessing. After all, Jordon worked for him. If Grey wanted to rehab in Pittsburgh, he damn well could, and he'd wield that power if need be. But he hoped it wasn't necessary.

He wasn't interested in demanding something from his agent—he wanted his brother's support.

The baby made tiny, mewling noises that made Jordon smile, and for a minute Grey put aside the conversation and simply enjoyed the view. Seeing Jordon with a baby was surreal. Seeing Jordon *comfortable* with something so small and needy was downright shocking. Jordon had never been the kind of guy who worshiped weakness. But as Grey watched his big brother gently rolling his son's tiny fingers between his own massive digits, he realized everybody at some point changed their mind about something.

"How long did it take you to really know Maggie?" Grey asked, sort of wondering aloud.

Jordon huffed. "You're not going to get me to fold by bringing up Maggie. Besides, we were different."

"How was it different? You'd been burned by Bethany and still you managed to trust Maggie enough to get married and have a kid." Grey reflexively raised his bandaged hand, gesturing to Braydon. He swallowed a massive rush of discomfort, because talking about these things didn't come natural—to either of them. He doubted he'd even attempt this conversation if Nel hadn't taught him that talking helped him make sense of what he was thinking.

"Maggie didn't come after me. I went after her."

"Nel didn't come after me. She found the dogs and brought them home. It wasn't like I met her in some stadium-side bar."

"All I'm saying is you haven't known her very long."

"How long did you know Maggie before you knew she was… you know…the one?"

Jordon settled back in his chair, hoisting Braydon to his shoulder, adjusting the blanket wrapped around the boy. At first, his lips stayed pressed in a noncommittal line, while he glared at Grey, no doubt trying to find a way to turn this conversation around, because if Grey's hunch was right, the conversation would lead him to Pittsburgh and back to Nel again.

With an exaggerated sigh, Jordon spoke. "Maggie had been here about a month when I suddenly knew I always wanted her to be here when I came home. Of course, convincing her to *be* here was another story, and it wasn't easy, but it worked in the end." He smiled as he rubbed the baby's back, and when he noticed Grey grinning at him, he growled. "Fine. I admit there's some element of risk involved with relationships no matter how long and who it is, but by God, you need to be careful. You need to be sure."

Was he sure?

Grey imagined Nel in his house with his dogs. He imagined going home to them. And he was sure. Damn sure. *Sanctuary.* He didn't know exactly what the word meant, but it stuck in his head amid thoughts of her smile and easy calm in the face of his intense moods. She diffused him. She loved him. She completed him.

Grey straightened in his chair, preparing for a fight. "I *need* to rehab in Pittsburgh, J. I'm not asking you. I'm telling you."

A few agonizing seconds passed and Grey wondered if he was going to damage his relationship with his brother by not taking his professional advice yet again. But then a slow smile spread across Jordon's face, and he shook his head. "You know, I should've seen this coming. Maggie said she talked to you."

Grey grinned. "She asks a lot of questions; questions that make a man think."

"Tell me about it." Jordon stood, cradling Braydon's head, and then he crossed the deck to slide open the screen door with his free hand. "I'll catch up with you later. I have some calls to make."

Grey fidgeted. "So we're going to leave it like that?"

"Like what?"

"Without coming to an agreement about me rehabbing in Pittsburgh."

"Little brother, it's going to take more than an agreement between you and me. I need to talk to Buckhalter and ask him to oversee your rehab, knowing he's going to be stepping on some toes in Nashville. If he won't do it, then you're going to have to rethink this plan. Nothing's more important than your career, right?"

Grey used to think so. Now, he wasn't sure. If there was a way he could have both, then he was damn well going to find it, but if he was forced to choose…he'd choose Nel.

"Right?" Jordon asked again. "Think carefully about how you answer that." His brows waggled. "If you agree with me, then I'm going to have no choice but to think Pittsburgh is a big mistake, and I'm going to insist on you rehabbing in Nashville."

"And if I disagree with you, if I say there's something more important than my career?"

"Then I'm going to think you're in love, man, and I'm going to have no choice but to book you on the first flight to Pittsburgh. So let me ask you again, nothing's more important than your career, right?"

"Wrong," Grey said with a grin.

"Then get off your ass and let's get you out of here."

The grin stretched into a giant smile as Grey lifted out of the chair and followed Jordon into the house. He was going back to Pittsburgh—to Nel.

No plane on earth could get him there fast enough.

CHAPTER EIGHTEEN

Nel clenched her hands and swiped her tongue around her dry mouth as she stood on the front porch of the house across the street from Grey's.

She'd waited to make the short-but-agonizing trip until The Fortune Agency sign was yanked out of the front yard. But now that she was here, she battled the usual nerves that went along with cold calling, reminding herself the worst thing they could do was slam the door in her face. And while that would be bad, it wouldn't kill her—she'd survived a lot worse lately.

The door clicked and creaked, and an older man appeared on the other side. Bald with smooth skin, a slight frame, and wire-rims low on his nose, he smiled. "I don't suppose you're selling Girl Scout cookies, are you?"

"No," Nel said, smiling back, thinking a packet of Thin Mints was the perfect thing to calm her queasy stomach. But since she didn't have any, she rolled back her shoulders, lifted her chin, and took advantage of the opening. "While I don't sell cookies, I do sell houses." She nearly groaned at the cheesy segue.

Fortunately, the man didn't seem to mind. He slid the glass off his nose and chuckled. "Penelope Parker, I presume."

She startled at the use of her given name. "I go by Nel, but yes. How did you know?"

"I've been expecting you. Florence across the street called and said she was listing her house with you. She was pretty adamant I do the same. And let me tell you, I've lived here long enough to know Florence isn't one you want to cross." He chuckled again. "I'm Jack Lewis, and it's nice to meet you, Nel. Come on in."

Nel smiled, remembering Florence pointing out Nel's given name on the listing contract. "My mother's name was Penelope," she'd said with a wistful look on her face. The moment added a sense of kismet to their meeting. Just like this man expecting Nel added a sense of kismet to *this* meeting.

Some things were meant to be.

And some things weren't. She tried to block another onslaught of Grey-related thoughts, but they barreled through her defenses, making her words slow and stilted as she moved through the house, exchanging small talk with the man. How could it be that on the verge of having everything she ever wanted professionally speaking, a giant portion of her was empty?

They walked into a sunroom where an elegant older lady draped an open book over the arm of a couch and stood.

"Meg, this is Nel Parker, the real estate agent Florence was telling us about."

Nel reached out to shake her hand. "It's nice to meet you."

"Likewise, dear."

Over the next two hours, the couple gave Nel the grand tour of their gorgeous home and a figurative tour of the neighborhood, pointing out all the older couples who might be interested in selling. They explained their need to downsize due to rising medical expenses, and they plied her full of coffee and muffins.

And then they signed on the dotted line, giving Nel her second listing on Mulberry Run.

Grey's house would make three.

She should've been happier. But over the last few weeks she'd come to accept the hollow space in her heart, knowing it waited to be filled by Grey. She used to think whatever was between them was strong enough to linger through the rough spots, and rekindle whenever they managed to be together.

Only he'd stopped calling with any real frequency, and when he did there was a distance made of more than miles. That distance made her put less stock in overly romanticized ideas like being together—ever. At her weakest, she wished his dogs had never run in front of her car, giving her cause to meet him. But every once in a while—usually when she drifted off to sleep or was seconds from waking—it was like he was here again. And in those moments, she was whole. Pathetic…but whole.

Nel had no idea what the future held for either of them, but as long as she loved him, she hoped he'd wake up one day and realize he loved her, too.

• • •

The taxi slowed in front of the big stone house on Mulberry Run in Pittsburgh and for the first time in weeks Grey felt like he was home, like he belonged somewhere. And joy ripped through the scars in his chest.

His thank-you was a bit too exuberant for a crappy taxi ride, and his tip was overly generous, too, but he couldn't stop the flow of happiness bubbling up from the cracks in the misery that had overshadowed everything he'd done these last few weeks.

Because Nel was here.

Her car was in the driveway, parked next to his truck, and although he wasn't cleared to drive either vehicle, he'd never been happier to see a couple of cars. He hurried up the driveway to the walk, wondering if she saw the taxi, knowing if she did she was probably shocked, because he didn't tell her he was coming. He envisioned a big-screen-worthy surprise, complete with Nel running into his arms. But part of him worried enough time had passed for her to question her love for him, and if that was the case, there was a chance her reception would be lackluster.

When she didn't answer the door before he reached the stoop, he figured she hadn't seen him arrive—he hoped that was the case. His doubt grew with every breath. What if she didn't want him here?

With one hand, he fumbled the keys from his pocket and into the lock, leaning against the door to open it. The view on the other side stopped him.

It was perfect. Furniture he recognized from his father's gaudy collection was mixed with pieces he didn't recall, creating an oddly welcoming showplace. He closed the door and took a few steps into the great room, marveling at everything from the furniture arrangement to the pictures on the wall. It didn't feel like a Vegas mausoleum anymore.

It felt like home—his home.

Every last muscle in his body relaxed as he breathed in the woodsy scent of a freshly cleaned house, and he knew…coming here had been the best decision he ever made.

But where was Nel? He took a few more steps and decided surprising her was one thing, while scaring her was another. "Hello?" he called, when what he really wanted was to yell, "Babe, I'm home." He'd have to wait and see his reception before he started throwing phrases like that around.

And then came noise from the far side of the house. Grey's heart fluttered, because he knew what those uneven thuds meant. His boys were coming to greet him.

Blackjack and Joker burst from the hall amid a barrage of snorts. Hiding his right hand behind his back until the initial rush of excitement passed, Grey squatted to their level. It was pure chaos, and Grey couldn't stop smiling.

But where was Nel? Surely she heard the commotion. Unless she was in the shower or blow-drying her hair. Maybe she was getting ready for an open house. He stilled, listening over the dogs panting.

"Come on, boys," he said, standing. "Let's go find her." She had to be here. Her car was in the driveway.

He searched, which took longer than necessary, because every room offered another opportunity for him to marvel at the transformations Nel and her brothers had made in his absence. Even using half of what was already here, she managed to make it look and feel like she did; a casual beauty, an easy elegance. Nel's mark was everywhere he turned, but she wasn't here …

She'd be back, he told himself, trying not to obsess about where she might be on a Sunday.

The dogs clamored at his feet, with Joker dragging a shredded towel around behind him. The instinct to reach down with his right hand was still strong, despite weeks of little use.

Grey used his left hand to grab the loose end. He tugged once, and with a vicious shake of his head, Joker ripped the towel free. The dog brought it back, urging Grey with a nudge to the thigh to keep playing, but Grey preferred to avoid the painful reminder of his injured hand.

He walked on, and the dogs followed. When they reached the kitchen, Blackjack and Joker headed straight for the French doors, overlooking the back yard. They walked tight circles on the doormat, and Grey knew they wanted out…but he didn't want to go out. The bright yellow tennis ball taunted him from the patio. The dogs started to whine—he had to try. It wouldn't be the same with his left hand, but maybe it would be enough to keep them happy and give him some sense of accomplishment.

When he opened the doors, Blackjack bolted for the ball, bringing it straight to Grey. He took a deep breath and gripped it hard in his left hand, reminding himself it didn't have to be good enough to reach a cut-off man from centerfield—it just had to be good enough for the dogs.

He pulled back his arm and pushed through the awkward motion, releasing the ball at a point just above his head, watching it sail from his hand in a tailing motion. It landed in the yard next door, several feet from where Grey had been aiming. But the distance was there, and the dogs didn't seem to mind. A pleasant chill rolled up his belly and settled in his chest. He wasn't completely useless.

Joker crushed the ball in his mouth, barreling toward Grey with Blackjack on his heels. "Good boy, bring it," Grey called …

But the dogs ran right past him.

• • •

Nel panicked when she saw Blackjack and Joker running across the gap between Florence's yard and Grey's yard. When they disappeared behind the house, she sprinted across the street, heading straight for the backyard, trying her damnedest to figure how they got out. They couldn't open doors, and she hadn't left any open. Had she?

The answer stood with his back to her a few feet from the patio. The surprise of seeing him stopped her on the top cobblestone step, but her heart pounded and her muscles twitched in excited defiance. *Run to him*, said a voice in her head. But what if she was dreaming?

There was only one way to find out.

Nel opened her mouth to call his name at the same time the dogs saw her, careening around Grey, and charging her. She looked down for a moment, weathering their powerful nudges with a bend to her knees and arms around their necks, and when she looked up again—half expecting the vision to have evaporated— he was still there, looking at her.

"Oh my God," she said straightening, the dogs clamoring at her feet. "You're here."

His smile was guarded. "Is that a good oh-my-God?"

His left hand stuffed in his jean pocket, forcing one side of his black ski jacket behind him, showing off a snow-white T-shirt, pulling across the wide chest underneath. He was more beautiful than she remembered. A massive masculine presence softened by the hint of uncertainty that played out on his gorgeous face.

Words failed her, stuck someplace between her aching heart and her watering mouth, so with the dogs on her heels, she walked until she stood before him. On tiptoe, she took his face in her icy hands and lowered him for a kiss. For a second, she stilled—lips to lips—breathing in the warm, cinnamon air that flowed out of him. And then he clamped an arm around her waist, forcing her against his solid frame, changing the angle of his lips, applying a persuasive pressure that made her open her mouth and come undone.

He was here. Really here.

Heat slithered from the tip of her tongue, down her throat, to her belly, and a woozy fog thickened the meager thoughts in her head until she wasn't thinking at all…just feeling. His tongue sliding over her tongue, her breasts full and hot against his chest, his fingers tucking inside the waist band of her pants, making her hips arch in search of him.

"So what you're telling me is it was a good oh-my-God." His wet lips moved against hers, his words breathy.

"Very good," she managed, despite the overwhelming need to fuse her mouth to his.

He ran a hand the length of her back to her neck where he laced fingers into her hair. "Nel…" he pulled his head back further, the heavy-lidded eyes contradictory to his sweet smile. "…do not sell this house."

It was her turn to pull away. Her hands slipped from his cheeks to his shoulders, and she settled on flat feet.

"Why not?" she whispered, afraid to answer her own question because of the sheer amount of ridiculous hope pooling in her heart.

"I'm going to be here for a while."

Her heart hoarded blood, making her head a complete vacuum. Worse, she couldn't read him for answers. Half his face still darkened from the intensity of their unexpected tryst, and the other half was blank now that his smile had faded. "I don't understand…you need to start rehab."

"I can do that here. Jordon is working on the details."

Happiness sparked but didn't fire completely. She should be deliriously happy about this, right? But her happiness felt selfish, and she refused to indulge until she knew he wasn't making a mistake. She hadn't told him she loved him to make him choose.

"What about the team?" she asked. "They can't be too happy about it."

His shoulders shrugged beneath her hands. "They're not, but the way I see it, rehab is rehab, wherever I do it. And at the end of the day, if the hand doesn't get better, they're going to cut me, and I'll be leaving Nashville anyway." His cheek twitched.

"They can't do that."

He scoffed. "They can. I made it an easy option for them by getting a non-baseball related injury. It's in my contract."

"Oh." She hated that. She'd gone over and over the injury since it happened, wanting to strangle herself for falling asleep in the first place when she should've been awake, making love to him, avoiding the whole dire outcome.

He wrapped his hand around the bulk of her hair, lifting it off her neck in what felt like a makeshift ponytail, and then letting it settle in spine-tickling waves. "I don't want to talk about baseball. I want to talk about what comes after baseball."

Nel's body was a complete contradiction, buzzing with basic desire from being so close to him, and yet aching for the state of his career. "Don't talk like that. Baseball's not over. I refuse to believe that."

"I like the way you think," he said, brightening with a smile. "And I hope I have years left in me. I do. But at some point, I won't, and when that time comes, I want to make sure what comes next, comes next with you."

She gasped, and cold air tinged with him clogged her throat. If she was dreaming this, it would be the cruelest dream ever.

"I love you, Nel," he continued, sliding his hand to her cheek, smoothing his thumb across her lips, and smiling like loving her was all he cared to do. "It's a clumsy kind of love, because I don't have many good examples of the strong kind, but I figure if you saw past all that to love me in the first place, then we've got a pretty good shot at making this last."

She gasped again, because frankly it was the only way she was capable of breathing. There wasn't enough air getting to her brain to cause much more than truncated thoughts, so again, she kissed him, this time, throwing her arms around his neck and pulling him to her. *Sweet Baby Jesus.* Was it possible for a person to have everything she ever wanted?

He wrapped both arms around her waist, but only one palm flattened against her back. Her swelling bubble of joy sprung a leak. She wanted him to have everything he wanted, too.

With palms to his chest, she put a couple inches of space between them. "This will be no vacation, Kemmons."

He cocked a brow. "Excuse me."

"If you think I'll go easier on you than Jordon or anyone in Nashville, you're crazy. Under my watch, you're going to work harder and longer than you think you're capable of."

"So you're my physical therapist now?"

"No, but you just fired me from being your realtor. I need something else to do." She grinned.

"I'll give you something else to do." He wrapped her up and backed her toward the door, nuzzling his face into the crook of her neck, sparking the happiness to full flames.

They nearly tripped on the dogs heading into the house, but somehow they managed to stay upright.

When he lifted his face from her neck, he looked around with a smile. "You did an amazing job in here."

"Thank you. It's just a little staging." She turned in his arm to study the results of her hard work. "I can change anything you want me to change now that you're…staying." The word snagged on her tongue, like she couldn't believe it was true.

He pulled her to him and pressed a soft kiss to the corner of her lips. "It's perfect."

"Are you sure?" She was talking about so much more than the house.

Grey chuckled. "You sound like Jordon."

His brother couldn't possibly be happy about this. Nel still caught a chill when she remembered the way he treated her at the hospital. "What about Jordon? What about your plan to pay him back?"

"He said the best payback was me living happily ever after in this house…with you."

She smiled until her lips hurt. "I like the sound of that."

"So do I." He wrapped her up hard and warm against his chest.

Nel closed her eyes, melting into him, listening to his heart beating. Trying to make sense of what was happening. "I always thought you hated this house." The words muffled with her mouth pressed into the crook of his arm.

"You changed my mind."

She looked up, meeting his shining, smiling eyes, surprised to see colossal joy there, despite all he faced. She supposed love was to blame. It had a way of blocking out the bad and building up the good, of making people feel invincible.

"Well, would you look at that," he said.

"What?" She turned her head to see what he was referring to.

"The clock on the wall says you're on your lunch break."

"It's Sunday, and I'm off," she said laughing.

"Shhh." He dropped his mouth to within a mere heartbeat of hers. "Let's pretend it's Monday."

And they did.

More from This Author
(From *Save My Soul: Book One in the Kemmon Brothers Baseball Series* by Elley Arden)

Maggie blinked at the picture she held in her hand. She rubbed her eyes. She tilted her head. She even squinted. No matter how she studied the tattered square, the image didn't make sense.

Her date reached across the bistro table and flicked the back of the photo. "That's my wife and kids."

Maggie counted eight children. A PhD in counseling psychology couldn't guide her reaction. Years of embracing Buddhist dharma couldn't ease her shock.

"I'm sorry." She shook the fog from her brain. "You said ex-wife, right? I must've misheard you." Which wasn't likely. Psychotherapists knew how to listen.

A smile warmed Paul's brown eyes and brought out a dimple in his cheek. Maggie hadn't noticed the deep dip a week ago when he grinned from behind a farmer's market herb stand. She hadn't noticed a wedding ring, either. Glancing at his naked left hand, she felt relieved. There had to be a rational explanation for this irrational conversation.

"Katherine is my wife. We've been married for twenty years." The words leaped from his lips and pinned Maggie to her chair, snapping her bare back against the metal with enough force to sting.

She folded her arms over her chest and breathed, trying to plot a graceful exit from the alternative universe disguised as a coffee shop she must have landed in.

"It's time for another wife."

This was where desperation had led her. But as much as she loathed being a twenty-eight-year-old PhD living at home with her mother, Maggie wasn't desperate enough to escape by way of a married man. She might be liberal, forward-thinking, and even a little off-the-proverbial-wall, but she wasn't a home wrecker.

Drawing a shaky breath, she cursed the crowded location and leaned forward. "I'm sorry. You seem nice enough, but I can't be with a married man. Tonight was a mistake."

She reached into her patchwork purse, but before she fished out keys, Paul wrapped a clammy hand around her wrist. "Don't go. Let me explain. I have Katherine's blessing to pursue you."

"You don't have my permission," Maggie said, uninterested in the details.

He released her and slinked back in his chair, looking very much the misunderstood martyr with glassy eyes and tight lips.

A bolt of pity wrapped in sensibility struck her brain. *Deep breath, Maggie. Calm down.* After all, the evening was innocent. They hadn't even held hands. What harm had been done on a platonic first date?

Compassion caused her to smile. "Good night, Paul. Go home to your wife and kids."

"But I'm a polygamist. I want another wife, and Katherine wants a sister wife."

Maggie widened her eyes. Though rumor had it Salt Lake City overflowed with plural marriages, in the year since she'd moved home with Crystal, Maggie had yet to meet one. Until tonight.

Grabbing the edge of the cold table, she breathed through her nose and exhaled relief. Paul wasn't risking the wrath of karma by proposing an illicit affair. He was explaining an alternative lifestyle. While Maggie had no desire to be Wife Two, she owed him civility and the opportunity to communicate without humiliation. After all, she was an expert in interpersonal communication.

She nodded in understanding. "Please tell Katherine I'm sorry, but I'm not sister wife material. Thank you for the coffee."

Maggie lifted from the seat with as much grace as she could muster and scurried across the tile floor. Her feet wobbled in too-high heels, and her knees knocked below the hem of her flowing skirt. When she finally reached the exit, a cool rush of late October air layered her skin with goose pimples.

She'd been in a lot of ridiculous situations, but this may have topped them all.

Slamming the door of her Aquarius blue VW convertible, Maggie faced the fact that her date was a bust, and now she was going to have to drive home. Face her mother. Rehash the story when all she wanted to do was climb into bed.

This was not the life she expected to be living at twenty-eight. Then again, her entire life had been beyond normal expectations. When most mothers were teaching their daughters to read books, Maggie's mother was teaching her how to read auras. Inside their circle of friends, inside the safe haven of their bungalow, it was a skill no different than rolling her tongue. But out here, in mainstream society, it made Maggie weird, an outcast. She couldn't seem to fit in. Even the men she attracted were…different.

Maggie dropped her head to the steering wheel and groaned. Where was the balance? The ying and the yang? She'd worked hard to gain academic success and respect, in the process, hiding a big portion of herself and her upbringing. And where did that get her? Barely able to pay her student loan interest, car expenses and rent for her office space. This was "failure to launch" wasn't it? She was doomed to grow old, at home, alongside her aura-reading, spell-chanting mother.

But right now, Maggie couldn't go home. She couldn't face the woman who'd be waiting in the rocking chair. Sometimes a girl didn't need her mother.

She turned the key, firing the engine, not knowing where she was going. Her friends were polar opposites—spiritual seekers vs. mental health professionals—and yet both groups would agree

Maggie was struggling with self-discovery. What Maggie really wanted was a single friend who would line up shots and drink with her to oblivion.

She drove without direction, listening to the pathetic thoughts in her head until she tired of the wallowing and replaced her thoughts with a mantra. She whispered the words over and over again as she traveled tree-lined streets.

Eventually, her mouth stopped moving and thoughts started forming. The first? She had a decision to make. She couldn't live in both worlds. Either she embraced her mother's way of life or she moved out and carved life on her own. But between student loans, car expenses, and rent for her mostly unused office space, Maggie had only managed to save five hundred dollars since she moved back home. It wasn't enough money for a security deposit, let alone a down payment.

Passing her street, needing more time to think, Maggie guided the car down South Temple and stopped to let a ghost and goblin cross. In the chaos of the evening, she'd forgotten about Halloween. Glancing at her white knuckles, she wished she was younger, with hands wrapped around a pillowcase bursting with candy instead of strangling a steering wheel. Kids didn't know how hard life would get. They couldn't imagine there would ever come a time when they wanted to move out of the house and live life on their own. But Maggie knew, and knowing sucked.

With no other place to go, Maggie parked her Volkswagen in the driveway of a historic Victorian, disarmed security features at the back door and reset the system on the other side. She switched on a chandelier in the main hall and blinked at the brightness. Crystal always said, *look for the bright side*, but Maggie couldn't find a bright side when she was in the middle of an existential crisis.

She growled as she pounded her heels against the hardwoods and took the wool-covered stairs by two. At the east end of the wallpapered hall, she ducked into her office, shutting the six-panel door and driving a bolt lock into place. For a moment, she froze against the thick wood, but then an exhale carried her lanky body to a purple couch. She collapsed, face down on the purple velvet.

Reaching up without looking, Maggie switched on a glitzy lamp and turned her head. She opened her eyes to the Buddha that Crystal had placed against the far wall and the tapestry zafu that was a graduation present from Yogi Hajan. The pair would no doubt advise Maggie to meditate, but she couldn't muster an ounce of spiritual motivation. She looked away before the inanimate objects could guilt her further.

Her orange Macbook sat on the desk where she'd left it hours ago after a virtual therapy session. Maybe one of "her girls" needed help. Somehow it was easier helping other people face their emotional, spiritual, and familial crises than it was helping herself.

Maggie booted the computer and headed straight for Facebook. No new messages. Nothing lurked in her inbox either. Of course not. What sort of college kid stayed in and chatted with her therapist on Halloween night when there were fraternity mixers and costume parties to attend?

She typed a quick email to the small group of clients, detailing her open availability tomorrow. Via email, chat room, webcam or old-fashioned telephone, Maggie would listen to stories of binge-eating peanut butter cups and the bouts of purging that kept the troubled young women up all night.

Pain twisted her heart, and this time the hurt wasn't because of her own screwy life. Virtual therapy allowed Maggie to guide eight clients, battling eating disorders in different corners of the country. The technique was her focus in graduate school, earning her name recognition in scholarly journals near and far. Her avant-garde approach to therapy was something to be proud of, the one and only time she was able to mesh her alternative side with her professional side, resulting in vigorous accolades.

Maggie ran shaky fingers through her spiky hair and considered meditating again, but her thoughts were hijacked by a ringing cell phone. She blinked at the touch screen, expecting to see Crystal or even Polygamist Paul, not an unknown number. The twist of her stomach told her not to answer, but her brain overrode the unexplained nervousness. What if someone was in trouble?

"Maggie Collins," she answered.

There was a brief pause, followed by the deep rumble of a throat clearing. "Dr. Collins, this is Jordon Kemmons. I'm not sure if you remember me."

Her core temperature plunged and then skyrocketed. The skin on her arms pimpled, and tingles spread across her chest. "I remember."

How could she forget? Six months ago, his tan skin, black hair, towering stature, and ominous aura haunted her from behind the podium, where he addressed the graduating class of his alma mater—now her alma mater, too. He stirred such strong feelings in Maggie, she worried the neo-gothic buildings surrounding the commons would crumble after more than one hundred years of steadfast footing. But that was nothing compared to the unsettling jolt of their shared handshake when Maggie was awarded recognition for her research. Something about the darkly handsome man strangled her breath and drained her soul.

"I hope it's not too late to call. I work all hours and pay little attention to clocks and time zones. Can you talk or should we set another time?"

He didn't sound the least bit remorseful for the intrusion, and she had the intuitive feeling that he intended to have the discussion whether she was busy or not. A burst of nervous energy fluttered between her ribs.

"I happen to be at the office, so it's the perfect time to talk." About anything other than late-twenties life crises or polygamists and sister wives.

Maggie ditched her red heels and folded her long legs in the shape of a pretzel.

"You see patients on Halloween night?"

"Clients." How many times had Maggie explained to the layperson about the importance of choosing words wisely when it came to mental health? She sighed and reached for a rote explanation. "The word patient denotes sickness, and my clients aren't sick. They need options and guidance. And no, I'm not seeing clients. I'm doing…inner work."

Silence. She leaned forward, carrying goose-pimpled arms to her knees where her eyes caught the movement of a nickel-sized spider suspended from the blade of a ceiling fan.

"Dr. Collins, I have a proposition for you."

The spider plummeted toward her bare leg. She screamed and leaped across the room, panting into the phone.

"What?" he barked. "Are you all right?" His yelling vibrated her eardrum and flooded her body with foolishness.

She kept her eyes on the spider and one hand over her throbbing heart. "I'm fine. It's a spider." She drew a deep, cleansing breath. "I apologize for my skittishness tonight."

"Let me guess. You believe portals to the other dimension open at midnight on All Hallows Eve, populating the earth with immortals hungry for human souls."

Maggie balked. Was this guy serious? He had no idea how scary real life could be. "Immortals haven't even crossed my mind, Mr. Kemmons. I'm merely distracted with thoughts of polygamy, sister wives and the likelihood of nervous breakdowns in a person's mid-twenties."

More silence. Deeper silence. The kind that made a heartbeat echo.

The spider scurried up the arm of the sofa and then made a U-turn toward the floor. Maggie leaped onto a leopard print footstool.

"Dr. Collins, I'm the agent for a pitcher who flaked out during game six of the NLCS. My sports psychologists can't break through. I don't think he's eating, and I've noticed unexplainable scars on his arms. Obviously this isn't about pitching. The kid is crazy, but his high-profile image makes it difficult to seek inpatient treatment without career repercussions. Remembering your research, I thought maybe you could help."

Maggie winced and dug emerald green toe nails into the cushion, once again taking on the role as champion for the misunderstood. "Mr. Kemmons, the terms 'flaked out' and 'crazy' are offensive. People on a tormented mental plane don't deserve to have their temporary weaknesses belittled."

"Call him whatever you want to call him. I'll call it like I see it. And the way I see it, he isn't focusing. He can't throw a strike, and his fast ball dropped eight miles per hour. I can't negotiate a case of bats for him at that speed."

The spider disappeared under the sofa and reappeared on the woodwork. Maggie dropped her butt to the footstool and pinned her eyes on the eight-legged creature.

"I've exhausted all legitimate, medical treatments," he said with a huff. "Next up is reiki and some cranial sacral voodoo that a team trainer suggested. Before I toss Carlos off the deep end and jump after him, I figured I'd give your brand of hocus pocus a try."

Maggie winced. If he wanted the best hocus pocus money could buy, he'd have to call her mother.

Reaching up to calm a twitching vein in her forehead, Maggie rubbed her clammy skin. "I don't even know where to start," she said, releasing a sigh. "Reiki and cranial sacral therapy *are* legitimate treatments, neither of which do I practice. My brand of hocus pocus…" she choked a little on the words, "…is nothing more than tradition therapy offered in a non-traditional format. I'm sorry to disappoint you, but while I feel sorry for this boy, and not because he isn't pitching well enough but because he's forced to deal with your spiritual retardation, I'm hardly the person to help him heal."

Jordon snorted. "Did you just call me retarded?"

Maggie rolled her eyes, going over her words in her head. "Of course not. I simply meant your spiritual evolution is delayed."

"Is it now?" He didn't sound impressed.

She was beyond caring about impressions. Taking out the evening's frustrations on this faceless man seemed infinitely more enjoyable than beating herself up about it.

With a noisy exhale, Maggie released the frustration that had been locked inside of her since her awkward date with Paul. "Mr. Kemmons, every other word that comes out of your mouth offends me, and that's amazing, because I assure you, you won't find a more open-minded individual than me." She should've stopped there, but the emotional floodgate slammed open. "Just because I won't participate in a polygamist marriage or engage in orgiastic relationships doesn't mean I judge those who do."

Deep laughter slithered through the phone, tickling her ears and neck until it shot off tiny sparks in her chest. She pounded a fist against her breastbone to stop the tingles.

"Orgiastic." The way he said the word made her face burn. "I had no idea that was even a word."

She raised her hand, fanning the heat. "Never mind. I…Good night, Mr. Kemmons."

"Wait," he yelled. "I'm prepared to double your salary."

She didn't have a salary. She worked off billing and sliding scales. It was "eat what you kill," so to speak. And with her brand of therapy in low-demand, Maggie was starving.

"Dr. Collins, are you still there?"

Another shaky breath. "I am."

"Carlos plays for Carolina, and he's staying at my vacation home in Lake Norman. I'd like to pay you for a professional visit.

Talk to him. See if you can help. Travel and hotel expenses will be covered."

For a moment, all Maggie could see was a couple days away from a life that was closing in on her, and some extra cash to start anew. But when she opened her mouth to agree, her stomach clenched. If only she didn't feel like she was making a deal with the devil …

The spider scrambled in the distance, and Maggie scooted the footstool closer to the door.

"Are you interested in the opportunity, Dr. Collins?" he asked in a clipped and clearly exasperated tone.

Maggie had never been one to ignore opportunity, partly because she had her mother's impulsive streak, but also because she was smart and determined…and right now, she was struggling to make sense of her life. This opportunity could be key.

"Send me the terms in writing." She spewed the sentence before she could take it back, using as much conviction as she could muster.

The spider raced toward the footstool, and Maggie screamed, skipping across the hardwoods on tiptoes before she crashed into the sofa.

"What now?" he growled.

"The spider." She panted, waiting for the eight-legged demon to regroup and charge again.

"Kill the damn thing."

"No! That robs us of the chance to grow on a spiritual path. I practice a non-harming way of life, and I'm going to deal with this arachnophobia like any other enlightened adult. When I hang up, I'll talk to him."

Dead silence mixed with the distinct feeling that she said something wrong. Maggie knew the words that made sense to her sounded strange to everyone else—especially tall, dark, analytical men, but she couldn't help herself. Try as she might to tame her alternative thoughts, in times of duress they overruled.

She fought the urge to hang up and handle her mortification in private. "Mr. Kemmons, are you there?"

"I'm *all there*. I was about to ask you the same thing."

She caught his dreadful double meaning, but couldn't blame him. After all, she told him she planned to spend Halloween night talking to a spider.

Palming her face, she drew a deep breath and refocused. "You may think of my person however you like, but professionally, I'm without reproach. I accept your verbal terms and await a contract."

He chuckled. "Good night, Dr. Collins. Give my regards to the spider."

•••

Jordon pulled square black eyeglasses off his face and pressed his head to the scrolled headboard his interior decorator designed for occasions like this. He worked a lot in bed. There was a time when the work related to his libido. These days, the only thing waking him was the BlackBerry charging on his bamboo nightstand or the cordless phone resting in his hand.

A few feet below his bedroom window, the New York City streets hummed, keeping him company through another long night. He bent his knees, bringing the laptop with Carlos Nunez's final stats closer to his burning eyes and pressed the phone to his ear.

The buzzing was displaced by one word, spoken dejectedly with a hint of Spanish accent. "Hallow."

"Hey, buddy. How are you feeling tonight?"

"The same."

Jordon squeezed his lips until they hurt. When Carlos sniffed on the other end, Jordon thought about hopping a flight to Carolina so the kid didn't have to suffer alone. "Is Bernie there?"

"Just left." A yawn filtered through the receiver.

"Okay. Try to get some rest while I work on Plan B." Or was it Plan Z at this point?

Jordon smacked his head against the bed. If he had to, he'd start all over at Plan A and rework every detail until somebody, somewhere, helped this kid. "Night, buddy."

"Night…"

Dad. Jordon couldn't remember when it first happened, but for years now—maybe since he started down the hill toward forty—the name appeared in his head at the end of certain calls. For many of the young men he represented, the moniker wasn't far off. Jordon did more than guide their careers, and he sure as hell felt more for them than the average agent, which was precisely why Kemmons Corp. was anything but average.

Studying the laptop screen again, Jordon shook his head at the numbers. Last season, Carlos flaked out, but the kid wasn't a genuine flake, not like Dr. Maggie Collins.

You may think of my person however you like. Jordon clicked another browser tab and gazed on the exotic Maggie. Betty Boop eyes smiled at him from the pages of her website. He pushed a palm up the stubby underside of his chin, and a devilish grin crept across his lips. Oh, he liked. A lot.

The first time he saw her, she floated down a red carpet aisle, wrapped in traditional graduation garb—with the exception of those damn shoes. It took him a moment to remember he was presenting a doctoral award of excellence to the woman in fuck-me pumps. Later in the evening, at a graduate reception, they shook hands during an introduction, and Jordon momentarily lost his mind.

Glancing at his opening and closing hand, Jordon recalled the heat that travelled from her body to his. The physical attraction intensified when she joined a group in a belly-dancing tribute to an Egypt-bound professor. Having shed the scholarly robe, she wore a sleeveless dress that was little more than a slip. He remembered the generous amount of shapely leg between the hem of that so-called dress and the black bows tied around each ankle. Those tiny bows strapped stiletto heels to her feet as she rolled and swirled all over the dance floor like an erotic dream.

A dream he couldn't shake.

Snapping the laptop shut and tossing it to Bethany's side of the bed, Jordon slid down the headboard, pushed into the pillow and closed his eyes. The right side hadn't been Bethany's side for two years. He thought about rolling over, about reclaiming the space, but his back glued to the mattress. It pissed him off that he still couldn't sleep on the right side.

Maybe Carlos wasn't the only one who needed a therapist.

Jordon launched an exhale from his mouth to the ceiling. If Dr. Collins succeeded in fixing Carlos, maybe Jordon would modify his impression of her from flake to capable flake. The corners of his sleepy mouth lifted. Right now, though, the only impression he cared to imagine was how capable Dr. Maggie Collins was in bed.

ABOUT THE AUTHOR

Elley Arden is a born and bred Pennsylvanian who has lived as far west as Utah and as far north as Wisconsin. She drinks wine like it's water (a slight exaggeration), prefers a night at the ballpark to a night on the town, and believes almond English toffee is the key to happiness. Elley writes provocative, contemporary, series romance for Crimson Romance. For a complete list of Elley's books visit http://www.elleyarden.com.

In the mood for more Crimson Romance?
Check out *Rock Him*
by Rachel Cross
at *CrimsonRomance.com*.

www.ingramcontent.com/pod-product-compliance
Lightning Source LLC
Chambersburg PA
CBHW010304100726
47904CB00011B/2737